The Kreepton
Chronicles

An Unofficial Adventure Based on the World of
Minecraft

ᴓᴦᴦᴦᴦᴦᴦᴦᴦᴦᴦᴦᴦᴓ

Story and Art by Renee Libra

ISBN 978-0-9984316-0-4

For my son,
who reignited my passion to be a writer

Table of Contents

The Kreepton Chronicles

Chapter 1:
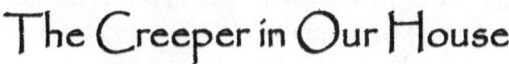
The Creeper in Our House

A lone creeper dwelled on our front porch.

How he came to adopt our porch as his home was quite fascinating. We found him collapsed in front of our house a moon cycle* ago, exhausted, injured, and covered in both old and new scars. Although he had the face of a creeper and his skin color was that signature green, he had a Human body with two arms and two legs. He wore an old and dirty overcoat that looked like it once belonged to a gentleman.

"Perhaps it's not really a creeper?" suggested Augusta, my survival partner and only friend in this world.

"Perhaps... but it could still be dangerous and explosive," I said.

"Well, Hadrian, look at it! It wears clothes! I think something sophisticated enough to wear clothes is capable of reasoning." Augusta was always the sympathetic one.

Augusta and I had been in this world as long as we could remember, but we never knew where we came

---

* A moon cycle is a reference of time. It is the number of days it takes for the moon to go from one new moon to the next, which is eight days.

from. We built our house with the wood gathered from the spruce trees that grew in the area. Wheats, carrots, and potato grew in a small farm next to our house. We also kept a few sheep and pigs for food. Occasionally, we would head to the nearby caves to mine for materials.

Life was routine and simple. The most extraordinary thing that could happen was when mobs showed up. We fought them bravely with great team work. The possibility that our visitor could be an intelligent life was certainly a welcomed thought. At the least, his presence brought some sparks to our, otherwise, dull existence.

It seemed that Augusta was right about this creeper being sophisticated. We spent a few days nursing him back to health, and when he finally was strong enough to get up, he opened his mouth and gave us a "Thanksss you."

"You can speak?" I was surprised.

"Ssertainly," the creeper answered calmly. "My name iss Kresstan."

"You haven't eaten since we found you, are you hungry?" asked Augusta.

"I would like sssome sssand, pleassse," Kresstan requested politely.

From the storage, we pulled out a few blocks of leftover sand we had from making our windows. Within clicks, Kresstan sucked them all up like a vacuum.

"BURRRRRRP......!" Then he let out a rather loud and satisfying burp. "Oh! Excussse me!"

We laughed for a good few clicks.

∞ᘉᘉᘉᘉᘉᘉᘉᘉᘉᘉᘉ∞

After a few more days of rest, Kresstan had regained

all his strength and was able to head outside to stretch out his limbs.

Although he spoke with an accent full of "s", he had proven himself to be a master of the Human language.

"I cannot thank you two enough for assisting me in my greatessst need!" Kresstan gave us his thanks with a deep bow like a knight for like the hundredth times.

"Again, Kresstan, you are very welcome!" I replied.

"I truly enjoyed my ssstay here, but I must now go," said Kresstan.

"And where will you be going?" asked Augusta.

"Continue to wander in thisss world asss I've done all thessse time," answered Kresstan in a sad tone.

"Why don't you stay with us for a little longer? If, you are not in any hurry," I offered.

"I...I...But...I ssshould not be a burden to you any longer."

"Oh! Don't try to be polite anymore, Kresstan! We'd love to have you here with us for a bit longer!" Augusta reached out and took Kresstan's scarred hand.

"We certainly need some time to fix those clothes of yours," I added, pointing to his worn-out leather overcoat.

"How could I deny such generosssity?" Kresstan showed undeniable gratitude. "But I inssist you assign me choresss, for I would not feel right to abussse your hossspitality."

"That is settled then." I smiled.

"We need to build a room for you..." Augusta looked around our eight by eight modest house to find a spot for a new room.

"That's not necessary," he said. "I prefer sssome fresh air outside and I don't really sssleep."

"In that case, the front porch is all yours." I said.

In no time, Kresstan transformed our once simple front porch into a comfortable little corner for himself. He meticulously crafted an armchair out of spruce wood and covered it with blue wool carpet. Next to the armchair, he placed a chest that contained a few of his belongings and gears and tools he crafted for his use.

In the next few moon cycles that followed, Kresstan helped us with farming, gathering coal, mining iron, making tools, and even designing traps around our house to capture any mobs that came too close. We spent so much time talking and laughing together that even his "s" accent seemed to have minimized, except when he got angry or excited—particularly when our conversation touched the topic of creepers.

Kresstan drew a very clear divider between himself and the regular exploding creepers that larked in our world. He, in fact, had an exceptionally strong disliking of them.

"Treacherousss traitor rebelsss!" he called the other creepers.

He hissed at all the creepers that dared to approach our house and it certainly kept them away for good.

"Creepersss are those armlessss exploding maniacsss out there!" Kresstan told us. "I may share some features with those foul creatures, but members of my kind are intelligent and well-mannered beings known as Kreeptons."

"Kreeptons!" Augusta caught on to our discovery. "I knew it! We are not the only ones with sense here!"

"Are they the reason why you ended up in the horrible state you were in when we found you?" I wondered. "Is that why you hate them so much?"

"They were part of the reason. A group of us was chased by dozens of mobs sent forth by our enemies and

I was separated from the others," Kresstan said with intensity. "I fought those mobs until my old sword broke and I was forced so far away from the desert that I ran out of food, too. I was very fortunate to have gotten away, but I was near death when I collapsed at your mercy."

"Well, I'm glad we found you in time!" said Augusta.

"Indeed, I was lucky to have survived and saved by your kindness," Kresstan replied with a smile.

"Do you have any idea where the rest of your group is?" I asked.

"I am afraid for the worst for the others," Kresstan's mood took a downturn.

In an attempt to lift up Kresstan's spirit, Augusta timely changed the subject. "May I take a look at that sword you have?" she pointed to a shiny sharpened iron sword with a birch wood handle hanged in an item frame.

"Oh... Most certainly," Kresstan came back to us from his painful memories.

"So nicely crafted!" Augusta admired.

"Thank you," said Kresstan.

"Do you mind if I see that chest plate, too?" I joined in, gesturing to an iron chest plate with a small crest carved on the center.

"Of course." Kresstan handed me his plate.

I examined the crest that looked like a gem with a creeper face placed over a tower of some sort. I have seen that crest before. "What symbols are these? The crest is the same as the one on your overcoat."

"It's my family's crest. The symbols represent the most important relics of our civilization." He gently touched the design. "I'm from a family of great warriors... That was another lifetime... I'm likely one of

the few of my kind that still exist, if not the last."
Kresstan looked blankly into the night sky, drifting into
the past once more. There seemed to be so many secrets
hidden in his deep hollow black eyes.

"Oh, I'm sorry, I didn't mean to disturb you," I
apologized while Augusta elbowed me for upsetting our
guest again.

"That's alright," Kresstan said calmly. "Maybe I
should tell my tale before I, too, perish in the hands of
my enemies."

He took a deep breath. Then he proceeded to tell us
a story so unexpected that it made us rethink our
existence in the world.

Chapter 2:
The Block World
Before Now

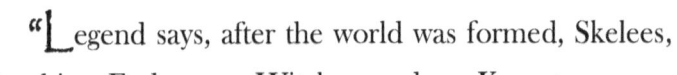

"Legend says, after the world was formed, Skelees,
Zombies, Endermen, Witches, and we Kreeptons were
spawned into the world." Kresstan lowered his voice and
began his story in a serious tone. "We were all creatures
of intelligence. And 'Humans' were unheard of."

It was quite intriguing to hear that those mobs could
do anything else but destructions, let alone be intelligent.

"Did they live in peace?" Augusta asked.

"Absssolutely not," Kresstan continued. "Each group of creatures claimed a territory and conflicts were frequent as each wanted domination over the others. Eventually, war broke out. Alliances were formed to gain advantages, but were broken again and again. The Endermen, for example, used the Witches to help them create the Ender Dragon, then turned around and hunted the Witches with the Dragon."

"The Endermen were backstabbers!" I exclaimed.

"Yes, they were," he agreed. "But the Witches didn't go down without a fight. Before they were hunted to near extinction, the few remaining Witches used their magic to trap the Endermen and their Dragon in another dimension known as the End. Only the few who possess the Ender Pearl could roam free in the Overworld."

"So, that was how they ended up there," Augusta realized.

"After countless moon cycles of fighting with weapons, magic, alliance, and betrayal, the Kreeptons emerged victorious and became the rulers of the world," Kresstan declared proudly. "We named our world 'Tallect.' Those proven loyal to the Kreeptons were allowed to share Tallect with us."

"There was peace in Tallect then?" I asked.

"For a while, there was," Kresstan exhaled, his eyes glowed when he tried to remember the happy times he had. "We built an amazing civilization out of sand, the source of our energy."

"Sand? Like a Desert Temple?" Augusta wondered.

"Desert Temples were one of those ancient constructions built by the Kreeptons," confirmed Kresstan. "And I was spawned into existence in one of those Temples. It was shortly before the Creeper Wars began."

"The Creeper Wars!?" we exclaimed at the same time.

"Those were the Wars that reduced our once great civilization into a desert," Kresstan said dimly. "And I spent a good deal of my life being a part of those Wars. Sadly, I don't think the Wars would end until all the Tallects are either captured or killed."

"How awful!" I pictured in my head the heartache our friend had to endure. "What happened?"

"Tallect was invaded by surprise," Kresstan organized his thoughts and continued. "Kreeptons are great inventers. After studying extensively the elements of the Tallect world, our scientists invented gunpowder. It was incredibly useful in our mining expeditions and allowed us to obtain a lot of materials with one explosion."

"The substance is, nevertheless, very dangerous. So, in order to mine deeper and prevent injuries from explosion accidents, we also crafted a vessel that can carry the gunpowder far away from the miners and into tight spaces. Each of these vessels consisted of a simple control center head that allowed it to navigate and find its target, a body that carries the gunpowder, and four quick moving short legs."

"THE CREEPERS!" lightbulbs came on in our heads.

"Yes, the creepers," Kresstan said darkly. "However, a useful tool can become a dangerous weapon when it falls into the wrong hands. Invaders who came out of nowhere somehow stole our mining invention and turned it against us!"

Kresstan stopped and looked down for several clicks to reflect on the miserable chapter in their history. The air was so tense that we were afraid to speak or even take a breath. When Kresstan lifted his head back up, his dark eyes were full of emotions. He spoke again.

"It was the day of my Right of Passage celebration. I was acknowledged as a grown and responsible Tallact, as well as the heir to my family's legacy. A storm was ravaging that night, but that didn't stop my family from hosting a grand party in my honor at the Capital City. Then just as the party came to an end, it happened..." Kresstan's voice lowered further. "The silent assassins... Those waves of creepers were sent into every corner of our cities in the dark of the night. Under the order of the invaders, the creepers ignited themselves throughout our city. The sound of crumbling buildings and desperate cries of citizens erupted in the night."

"Following the attacks, many were killed or injured. Much of our cities were destroyed. Our world descended into chaos. Those who were able to fight regrouped and built simple forts to defend ourselves. We gathered all the strength we had left and went to war. But the damages done to our civilization were too great and the time of peace had weakened our warriors. We were quickly overwhelmed by the invaders. Ultimate defeat followed. My whole family perished, along with hundreds of Tallects. We lost all our forts and the last of the survivors scattered far away from our cities."

"That is horrible..." Augusta frowned at the tragic story.

"But the invadersss did not stop there," Kresstan clenched his fist tightly in anger. "Their band of highly-skilled Master Hunters were sent to capture any remaining Tallects at large. I was leading a small team of Tallects in search of survivors when some Hunters caught up to us. My group sacrificed themselves to allow my escape..."

Kresstan went quiet.

"I'm sorry, Kresstan." I did not know how to comfort our friend.

"I'll be alright," replied Kresstan with all the calmness he could muster. "Please allow me some time to myself."

We went to bed quietly that night, leaving Kresstan to his memories of the past.

Chapter 3:
The Chronicles in the Chest

For a few moon cycles, Kresstan kept to himself mostly. He still helped us with our chores but he wasn't as cheerful as before he told us his story. Some days, he looked up to the sky, lost in deep thoughts. Some nights, he disappeared into the dark and came home just to get busy crafting, like he was preparing for a grand building project.

We had a lot in our minds too. If this world was once ran by Kreeptons and other intelligent beings, then where did we come from? We didn't recall anything before we spawned next to a river near these woods. And of the time we had lived here, we had not met a single Human. Were we the only Humans in this world? We didn't dare to ask Kresstan any more questions, for fear that it would send him further into his depressed state.

Then one day, Kresstan just disappeared without a word and his chest emptied. He took his armor, iron sword, and a load of mining tools with him.

At first, we thought he left us for good and grieved that we would never see him again. But five days later, we were relieved when we woke up to see him approaching our front porch carrying all sorts of materials.

He apologized for his sudden disappearance and explained that he needed some time to clear his mind and had to gather some materials to craft with. But even with the long absence and all those activities, his mood did not seem to change a bit. He continued to spend much of the days working by himself.

"We should have some kind of celebration, Hadrian," Augusta suggested one afternoon as we were cooking our lunch.

"To cheer Kresstan up?" I caught on to Augusta's idea. "The recent rain has helped our crops grow, so how about a harvest feast?"

"That would be perfect!" agreed Augusta.

"What's perfect?" Kresstan suddenly popped up behind us.

"Oh! Kresstan! You surprised us!" I said excitingly. "We are thinking of a harvest feast. We can bake some cakes and cookies. I found some cocoa beans the other day..."

"What if we have my farewell party instead?" Kresstan interrupted.

"Farewell party!?" We couldn't believe our ears.

"Yes, I believe it's time for me to go," Kresstan was determined. "My days here with you has been the best time I had in a long while. I'll truly miss your company.

But I'm afraid I have to undergo my quest."

"What quest are you talking about?" Augusta asked.

"I have discovered clues as to where other survivors may be." Kresstan explained. "If I can find them, we may still have a chance of rebuilding our civilization."

"That's...that would be good for you..." I was torn in my feelings about Kresstan's decision. On one hand, we wished that our friend would be able to fulfill his goal, but on the other hand, Augusta and I would be by ourselves again if Kresstan left.

"You won't be safe out there by yourself!" Augusta protested.

"I am not safe here either." Kresstan was firm like a commander. "You live simple lives here. My enemies will not rest until they capture, or worse, feed me to the mobs. I do not wish my friends to be in harm's way for my sake if that were to happen."

"How lucky it is to be your friends." Augusta came to know Kresstan to be one with a strong sense of duty to protect others. There was no point in trying to stop him. "When will you be leaving?"

"There's still some time before the conditions are right. And I also need to make some preparations."

"Let us help!" I offered.

Augusta nodded in agreement. "If your enemies are still out there going after you, won't you need some protection?"

"We are excellent swordsmen, too, you know!" I popped off an iron sword hanging on the item frame and performed a few swift moves to demonstrate.

"I have no doubt." Kresstan smiled. He, too, understood that we would not abandon a friend in need. "And I'm certain two extra pairs of hands will help me catch the deadline."

We wasted no time to begin constructing our plan. Kresstan cleared the table of our lunch dishes and replaced them with a stack of old journals.

"Are we supposed to read all these?" I would love to read a good story, but not this much!

"The reading has already been done. I've been studying them at night while you rested." Kresstan flipped through the journals looking for something to show us. "Shortly before those Hunters caught up to us, my team stumbled across a Desert Temple that was not destroyed during the Wars. In there, we found a chest containing these Chronicles detailing the events of the Wars. They were written after I set off to fight. Whoever wrote these observed a strange anomaly that took place on the night of the Creepers' attack—part of the Capital City vanished without a trace. Our scientists' research led them to believe that that part might have been transported into other existence, or another world."

"Another world!?" Augusta and I exclaimed.

"Ah, here!" Kresstan pointed to a passage written in words that made up of 'S's' in all sorts of fonts and pointing in all sorts of directions. That had to be the writings of the Kreeptons. "Upon careful examinations, they have uncovered the possible components that created the anomaly. If this is true, that must have been how the invaders get in and out of Tallect, too. I may also be able to find the Tallects that they have captured using this!"

"That's good news!" Augusta said.

"Indeed!" Kresstan continued reading. "According to this Chronicle, the spatial dynamics of the worlds are synchronized for a few short clicks every so often. Such synchrony would create massive thunder storms. If one were to capture the energy of the storm with a receptor, the worlds could be linked together temporarily and one would be able to travel between them."

"Sing-cro-knee and Dye-name-make?" Augusta lifted an eyebrow. "I'm totally lost on the science terms..."

"I'm no expert in that area myself," Kresstan admitted. "Though understanding the theory would not get me to the Tallects, but this 'receptor' would."

"So, what does this... 'receptor' look like?" I questioned.

Kresstan opened to a marked page from another journal. On it was a drawing of a tall plain pillar structure with a pyramid shaped top. A sword floated on top of the pyramid.

"This is called..."

"An Obelisk!" We both seemed to have recognized it at once.

"You know of it?" Kresstan was surprised.

"I...I'm not sure," I checked with Augusta. "Have you seen that before?"

"Feels like déjà vu," Augusta searched in her memory. "For some reason, I have an image of an Obelisk glowing in a dim light in my head... Perhaps it's my imagination?"

"That is very peculiar..." Kresstan's gaze lingered on Augusta for a moment as if he was suspecting something. Then he continued. "According to the records, the Obelisk is a tall lean sandstone pillar with a six by six base and fifty blocks tall. Four TNTs are placed in the inside corners of the base. A golden sword is placed on the very top with its blade pointing up. Redstone circuits connect the sword to the TNTs."

"That is a LOT of materials we need to gather!" I exclaimed.

"Well, I have done much of the digging, too."

Kresstan was proud of his accomplishments. "I took off for a few days to search for mines. From a particularly large mine, I managed to gather all those materials needed for the Obelisk."

So that was where Kresstan went when he disappeared for five whole days! Augusta and I were so amazed at Kresstan's mining capability, but we were even more amazed when he told us that he had actually seen this structure completed!

"It was the most sacred and ancient structure in the Tallect Capital City. Legend said that's where all creatures came into this world. And THAT was also the center where part of the city vanished. Upon careful surveying of the landscape, I have pin pointed the blocks where the original Obelisk stood using the positions of the stars and the writings in the Chronicles. It's only seven hundred blocks north of here. That's just half a day's journey."

"And all these time, we had no idea we were living so close to the Capital City!" Augusta said.

"Now, I've been wanting to ask," I said. "Are Tallects not capable of spawning new lives?"

"We do have that ability," Kresstan said.

"Then why aren't there new Tallects spawning?" Augusta asked.

"We Tallects need something called a Desert Crystal as our spawn point." Kresstan explained. "That Crystal was housed in the temple next to the Obelisk and it disappeared with that section of the City."

"In other words, no new Tallect can spawn into the world until the Desert Crystal is found," Augusta concluded.

"Exactly," Kresstan confirmed.

"Then, let's get to work!" I said. "What exactly do we

need to do?"

"In Short, we need to recreate all that was there that night."

"So you are saying if we build this Obelisk at the same location, and wait for the same conditions to happen, we could be able to transport ourselves into another world. There, we may find the other Tallects, and even the Desert Crystal?" I got excited.

"Simply put, yes," Kresstan confirmed. "But there's only a small window of time where the task could be accomplished. I've been studying the weather pattern as of late. If the data recorded in the Chronicles were correct, such massive thunderstorms we need happens every three hundred moon cycles, which would be four days from now, on the fourth Centum Moon Cycle Day of my birth."

"We don't have much time then," I realized.

Chapter 4:
The Obelisk Portal

The next day, after a quick breakfast, we packed some essential items like weapons, food, and all the materials needed for the massive construction. Kresstan emptied everything in his chest into his inventory.

We had one last look at our home and took off. Who knew if we would ever make it back.

With our swords at hand and ready to attack any mobs that might come our way, we headed north towards the desert.

"So, what else do you know about those who came after the Tallects, Kresstan?" Augusta asked as we were walking through the Savanna Biome.

"I've never seen their leader, but his Hunters called him King Steve."

"King Steve!?" Augusta and I baffled in unison. That name sounded very familiar, and yet, we could not seem to recall anything about this King Steve.

"The Tallects prefer to call him the Tyrant," Kresstan added.

After crossing the twenty-block wide river, we stepped foot on the edge of a sandy beach. A lonely torch on the horizon faintly flickered in the vast lifeless desert ahead.

"OK, now, where do we start?" I asked.

"The sun will be setting soon, we need to start building the base of the Obelisk around that torch to serve as our shelter for the night." Kresstan ordered.

"It's hard to believe that this empty desert was once the great city of the Tallects." Augusta said angrily as we treaded across the sand dotted with sandstone ruins. "Damn that Tyrant King Steve for destroying all that!"

Temporary storing away our emotions, we focused on our task at hand and started the construction right away. We lighted the premises with no less than thirty torches. It was so important that we secured the Obelisk so that no mobs would be able destroy our work as night descended.

The rest of the day was productive. With the three of us working, the Obelisk was already fifteen blocks high by sun down.

Augusta and I turned in for the night inside the half-completed Obelisk, while Kresstan stood guard in case of a mob attack.

Just a little more, and Kresstan would be on his way to be reunited with his kind.

Construction progressed smoothly without distraction. By the third day, we completed the whole Obelisk with even a day to spare!

"The last TNT is armed," I connected the last of the red stone dust to a TNT.

"Now, the only element we need is an electrical surge from a lightning," Kresstan consulted the Chronicles.

"Just wondering," Augusta asked while we put on a few finishing touches, "if the Obelisk had been there since ancient times, how come it never sent anyone to another world before the Creepers attacked?"

"The explosion was the key." Kresstan placed another sandstone. "After all, no one would destroy an ancient structure. But that night, the lightning during the storm ignited those invading Creepers, causing the explosions, and hence, activated the ancient Obelisk."

"So, once we blow this thing up, we won't be able to make another trip for another three hundred moon cycles?" Augusta asked.

"Seems like that would be the case," Kresstan said sadly. "I will certainly miss you."

"Wait! We are not going with you?" We were so busy building that we had not discussed our plans after the Obelisk was completed. But I definitely was not ready to say goodbye.

"I do not want to send you two into the unknown," Kresstan said. "This Obelisk design is in theory only. I trust the Kreepton scientists completely, but there are no records of what happens after one gets to the other world."

"I'm up for an adventure!" I said. "Besides, I have a feeling that we would find out about our own origins! How about you, Augusta?"

"I don't know about an adventure, but I'm not thrill to leave Kresstan to the unknown." Worry was written all over Augusta's face.

"Then it's settled! We are coming with you!" I announced.

"My effort of trying to stop you would most likely be wasted, my dear friends," Kresstan gave us a gentle hug.

We spent the last day gathering all the supplies that we may need to make the journey to the other world. Then again, how much could we prepare for a journey to the unknown?

In the evening of the fourth day, just after sun down, thick layers of clouds started to cover the once clear sky. Lightings were striking a few mountain tops in the distant, and they were getting closer by the click. We knew the time had come. We suited up in our iron armors and readied our swords. Kresstan put on his overcoat over everything. Using the ladders we crafted, we climbed onto a platform half way up the Obelisk to keep a distance from those TNTs for safety.

There, we waited for the lightning to strike.

"Alright, Kresstan, if we don't survive this, I just want you to know I'm happy to have met you!" I said with the amplifying rumbling of the thunders in the background.

"My thoughts too, exactly!" Augusta added. "And Happy Centum Moon Cycle Day, my friend!"

"Thank you. I'm happy to have met you, too." Kresstan smiled.

We felt a thunder going off right next to us, sending

a vibration down the Obelisk.

"It's time."

The red stone dust began to glow brighter. The next click, there it was—a lightning struck the sword on the top of the Obelisk. The electro power set off a chain reaction down the four strips of red stone dust, down to the four TNTs in each of the corners of the Obelisk.

BOOM! BOOM! BOOM! BOOM!

Four explosions went off simultaneously! A bright light enclosed the three of us. Am I supposed to feel pain for that much explosives? But I did not seem to feel anything in particular... My body went numb... Then my sight went blank.

Chapter 5:

Zombies in the Other World

How much time had passed?

Were we dead?

I couldn't feel a thing and I couldn't see either.

Where were Augusta and Kresstan?

My surroundings began to materialize...

Where were we?

A forest?

"Zee!"

I heard a faint voice?

"Woof!"

A bark?

That was interesting...

As my vision cleared up, I saw, about fifteen blocks away, a simple wooden hut enclosed by wooden fences in a forest clearing. A full-grown zombie was defending itself with a wooden shovel against a hostile dog barking just outside the fences.

"Zee!" The zombie called as the dog kept launching itself towards it. "Hurry up in getting the pork chop!"

The zombie talked?

Why was it not burning under the sun?

A child-sized zombie emerged from the hut with a pork chop. It tossed the meat a good twenty blocks away into the dense forest. What a strong arm this little zombie had! The dog chased the pork chop and disappeared into the woods.

"Great work, Zee!" the zombie praised. "Now let's

get inside before it comes back...Oh, my rotten flesh!"

The zombie spotted me.

"More Humans!" The zombie panicked. "Kneel, Zee! And beg for mercy!"

The zombies kneeled and kept their heads down. I stumbled to get back on my feet and was barely able to keep my balance. I was more so at their mercy!

"Hadrian?" Augusta's voice appeared behind me. Thank the Masters of the Blocks, she was OK! "Are those zombies...talking?"

"They *are* talking Zombies!" Kresstan emerged from behind a bush. "Though I haven't seen one in a while. They too were hunted down by the ruthless King Steve."

"Kresstan!" We all survived the blast!

"My rotten flesh! They have a Kreepton servant with them too!" the adult Zombie, a female one, mumbled in fear and bowed down her head even lower. "Please forgive us, we didn't mean to interrupt your hunt."

"No fear, my rotten friends, we are not hunters and I'm no servant. These Humans are my friends." Kresstan approached the rotten pair and extended a hand. "Please rise. I'm Kresstan. What are your names?"

"I'm Zella and this is my son, Zee." The Zombies looked up and began to stand just as Zella noticed the overcoat on Kresstan. "That crest...Kresstan...My rotten self! If it isn't the honorable Prince Kresstan!" Zella dropped back on her knees in a nano-click and pulled Zee down with her.

"Prince...Kresstan!? Your surprises are endless!" Augusta and I were shocked to learn yet another secret behind that green face. "That explains all the fancy talk!"

"On your feet, you two, I'm no prince. Not when I have failed the Tallects." He helped the Zombies up and turned to address us with a sense of shame. "I lost that title long ago when our civilization was destroyed."

"Well, we have more pressing matters to discuss." Kresstan returned his attention to Zella. "May we request your help in assessing our positions? We seem to have been taken to unfamiliar grounds."

"Of course!" Zella gave a bow. "Please come inside before that dog comes back."

The Zombies' hut was simple and everything was made out of wood. It was only four-by-four in size with a small fence windows on the opposite wall of the doorway. Inside, they had only a crafting table, a spruce wood table, two chairs, and all kinds of tools—some I did not have the slightest idea of what they were for.

"Zombies are masters of woodwork like Kreeptons are with our inventions," Kresstan pointed out. "They are also incredibly strong."

All five of us being in the hut was quite cramp.

"I'm so sorry. We don't really get visitors." Zella felt embarrassed for mistreating the prince.

"That is just fine. We can stand," Kresstan said in his full regal elegancy. "I'm simply honored to be in the home of some familiar faces."

Once we settled down, Kresstan began inquiring our location. "Is this, by any chance, still Tallect?"

"No, it's not..." Zella thought for a click. "You meant to say you came from Tallect!? Like through those Obelisk portals?"

"Yes. We have found a way to make that journey. And looks like it worked and brought us to you. And judging from your reactions, I assume you have also experienced the marvel."

"We have! Our captors took us to this world using a particularly powerful Obelisk," Zella recalled. "That is incredible! I never thought someone would figure out how it is done!"

"It was technology left by the ancients hidden in plain sight!" Kresstan referred to that Obelisk that once stood in the center of their Capital City. "Our scientists found out how it works during the Wars, but it was too chaotic of times to even let anyone else know about it."

Kresstan told the Zombies of how he discovered the Chronicles and how we built the Obelisk. Zella was so impressed that she even hoped that perhaps they would be able to build one here and finally return home.

"That is a comforting thought." Kresstan gave a warm smile. "But for now, let's focus on our current situations."

"Alright, of course!" Zella oriented herself.

"Mountains, rivers, forests... This looks very similar to Tallect," I observed, looking out the small window into the wilderness.

"If you are referring to the home of the once rich civilization of the Tallects, sadly, it's similar but it can never be our Tallect." Zella's tone was sad. "This world is ruled by the Kingdom of Geb, it belongs to the Humans. Or rather, King Steve."

"King Steve's world?" Somehow, we ended up in Kresstan's enemy's world. I don't know if that's horrible or great since we didn't need to travel any more to find this tyrant king.

"Wait a second...Humans? King Steve?" Augusta suddenly realized. "King Steve is Human?"

"He IS, beyond a doubt!" Zella said with disgust, but caught herself addressing two Humans. "My deepest apologies! I really didn't mean to offend. I...I..."

"Don't panic," Augusta gave her a pat on the shoulder to calm her, "we are not like King Steve."

"But wait a click..." a question popped up in my head, "Kresstan, were you, by any chance, hunted by Humans?"

"Yes, I was," said Kresstan, detecting where I was getting at.

"Then, why trust us? We could very well be your enemies," Augusta expressed our curiosity.

"But you aren't." Kresstan was very certain of his ability to judge a character. "If you were, from the moment you found me, you had ample chance to finish me off. Yet, you didn't."

"That...is true," I said.

"Back to the subject," Kresstan wasted no time in getting back to business. "Tell us about this world and all that King Steve has done to our kinds."

"Certainly, your highness... I mean, Mr. Kresstan," Zella chuckled with joy. She was still bathing in her good fortune of having the former Prince in her house. But given the urgent circumstances at hand, she quickly swapped her happiness out for a more suitable serious tone. "Geb is King Steve's home world. From what I've heard, he was a no-body before. But then he learned the secret of the Obelisk. Tallect was the first world he traveled to and he was determined to claim it as his own. And with the riches of Tallect, he gathered the power to put himself on the throne."

"He knew our intelligent kinds would fend him off if he just come in and steal our resources," Kresstan crunched his fist tightly. "So he sent in the Creepers to cripple us and hunted us down like scared animals!"

Anger filled Zella and Kresstan. Their home was destroyed because of one man's greed and ambition. Little Zee tried to comfort his mother with a hug.

No words could describe our disgust at King Steve's

cowardly tricks. Our conversation was drowned by a tidal wave of wrath.

Chapter 6:
The King's Secret

I finally broke the uncomfortable silent that seemed to last forever. "Are there any other survivors of your kinds?"

"Yes. King Steve's Hunters continued to search and capture any survivors they found," Zella answered. "He enslaved those who surrendered and threw those who defied him to the Creepers. Prince Kresstan must have been one difficult target for the Hunters to capture!"

"Don't flatter me, Zella. And no 'prince,' just Kresstan." The once royal Kreepton smiled warmly. "And what happened to the Tallects who surrendered?"

"We are separated by our kinds and placed in different parts of the Kingdom," Zella described. "We Zombies live here in the Western Forest and work as wood crafters. We make all kinds of wood products for the Kingdom. The Skelees are gathered in the Southern Mines and are miners and crafters of gold and iron. The Kreeptons live in a settlement near the King's Castle under heavy guard. The King employs them as scientists. Even he cannot deny their intuitions in technology."

"What of the Witches?" Kresstan asked.

"The Witches!" Zella suddenly became agitated at the mentioning of the potion makers. "They are traitors! They were the ones who provided the Tyrant with our Creepers! And as a reward, they are now part of the Kingdom's Council and have the authority as the King's advisers!"

"I should have known!" Kresstan could barely control himself as he learned of the treachery. "King Steve's Hunters seemed to know everything about us and knew just where to strike!"

It was one thing to have an outside enemy destroying your world, but when it was one of your own that led to your downfall, that was a whole other story.

Just then, we heard some voices coming from the outside.

"It should be here somewhere!" one of the voices said.

"Those rots are going to pay for tricking my precious puppy!" said another voice.

"Woof!" their dog echoed.

"It must be that dog earlier, and its owners!" Zella panicked. "Hurry! Hide! You can't be seen!"

"Where can we hide?" I looked around the sixteen-square-block hut.

"Down here!" Zella moved the crafting table to review a trap door underneath and signaled us to go in.

"How about you? Those people out there are not friendly!" Augusta was concerned with what those people would do to Zella and her son.

"I know how to deal with them," Zella assured us. "Tallects always have a way!"

We quickly climbed down the opening into the dark space. Kresstan took out a red stone torch to dimly light up the space as Zella moved the crafting table back in place to cover the trap door. Then we heard the footsteps of Zella and Zee quickly migrated out of the hut.

It took a few clicks before our eyes adjusted to the darkness. The underground storage was bigger than I thought. It's the same size as the hut and housed three double chests. We made minimum movements and waited in silent.

After what felt like an eternity, the crafting table was moved and the trap door opened.

"Is everyone alright?" Zella poked her head down.

How glad we were to see her rotten mug!

"How did you get away?" As Zella climbed down to the storage room, Augusta examined her all over to see if she was injured. Zee remained upstairs as scout in case the hunters came back.

"Oh, a little bribing would do it!" Zella said with a smirk. "I begged for forgiveness and gave them a nicely crafted bow."

Zella put up a few torches to light up the storage room, then she proceeded to one of the chests and took out an expertly crafted bow full of beautiful decorative floral carvings all over its limb.

"Something like this one." Zella showed us her work with pride. "I always have a few of these handy, in case I run into trouble with the Humans. They always appreciate a fancy weapon to show off to their peers."

"That's amazing!" Augusta and I held this piece of art in our hands.

"It's a shame that the once proud Tallect had to resolve to begging!" Kresstan muttered.

"I have something even better for you... Mr. Kresstan." Zella reached in to another chest and pulled out a large map covering almost the entire floor. "It's a map of the Kingdom of Geb. A map is quite hard to come by for Tallects, let alone one this large."

"Impressive! That must be quite a risk you took to possess this," Kresstan applauded. Zella smiled proudly for her work was appreciated.

"A small number of Humans are, in fact, not happy with the way Tallects are treated, they've been working with the Tallects to form the Underground Network to gather useful information and materials right under the nose of the King."

"I'm so glad to hear that there are other Humans with a sense of justice," said Augusta.

"I couldn't agree more." Zella nodded to Augusta. She then pulled out a stick and traced a thin line surrounding all the constructions. "The Kingdom is one big city surrounded by forests on a giant patch of land stretching a thousand blocks in all directions. A tall outer wall made of stone enclosed the whole area. Beyond the stone walls is untamed wilderness that is full of mobs of all sorts—armless creepers, brainless zombies, and heartless skeletons. Those self-righteous Humans, like those you saw earlier, enjoy hunting those mobs as a sport."

We squished over to give space to Zella to move to another side of the map.

"Here's the forest we are in, and the mining camps of the Skelees to the South." Zella directed our attention to the different areas of the Kingdom. "The Human City is enclosed by a second layer of thicker walls with two gates opening to the forest—the Western Gate and the Southern Gate. And here's the Tyrant's Castle on the eastern edge of the City next to a cliff, the Kreepton Settlement is within this Garrison just across from the Castle."

"What is this blur on the north here?" I pointed to the part of the map where the image did not form passed a skinny straight connecting blocks.

"That would be Beyond the Northern Gate," Zella said in a mysterious tone. "The area is enchanted. Even a map cannot show what's there."

"It has to be something important then!" I said.

"It's said that that's where King Steve crafts his most powerful weapon for his military conquests," Zella speculated. "It's well protected by the magic of the Witches."

"We have to get in there to find out the Tyrant's secrets! There may be a way to defeat him and save the Tallects from this slavery!" Kresstan got fired up and was ready to take down a mob army this instant.

"I would die to help you, my dear Prince!" Zella declared. "But I don't have the slightest idea on how to get in there. I believe the Kreeptons in the Settlement would know how. I heard that King Steve had sent Kreepton scientists beyond the Gate to work on a project. It's just that we are prevented from communicating with the other Tallects."

"In that case, we'll head to the Kreepton settlement to find out more about the Northern Gate." Kresstan stood up and readied himself to go.

"You won't be able to get into the Settlement by yourselves!" Zella said. "It's like a fortress!"

"There must be a way!" Kresstan was eager to see his people again.

"I have a Human contact in the City, she may be able to help. I'll give you the directions to get to her shop... And take this talisman, it is our token in identifying members of the Underground Network." Zella handed us a wooden talisman with a craving of a flower that we don't recognized. "It's a Daffodil, a flower that exists here in Geb, a symbol of new beginning."

"Ok, then that's done." Kresstan started climbing the ladder to get out of the storage.

"And one more thing, you can't go into the city like that," Zella warned.

"Why not?" I asked.

"Tallects are not allowed to leave our designated areas of residence," Zella turned her gaze to us, "unless escorted by Humans for work..."

That just gave us an idea...

Chapter 7:
The Mischievous Inventor

It was already night fall when we finalized our plan, so we had to wait out the night.

The next morning, Zella dressed us up in special armors. An indifferent Human face the size of a hand decorated the center of the chest plates and the front of the helmets, marking us as soldiers of Geb. Zella received them from members of the Underground Network for undercover operations like this.

Those armors felt quite comfortable on us, like our bodies were naturally molded for moon cycles to fit them. Geb sure had perfected the armor making for Humans.

Augusta and I emerged from the Zombies' hut with Kresstan behind us. Our Kreepton companion sported his own outfits and carried a few wood carving tools Zella gave us as props.

"Please be safe." Zella walked us out just up to her fence gate, not daring to step out of bound.

We thanked Zella and gave Zee a pat on the head.

The hundred-block walk to the Western Gate was uneventful, but once we got close to the Gate, our hearts pumped faster. The Gate was wide opened, but it was hardly welcoming. Two tough-looking guards armed with swords stood on both sides of the opening. They stopped us as we approached.

"I don't remember seeing you going out the gate," one of the guards investigated.

"We went out from the Southern Gate to the mines before we went to the Zombies for some wooden tools," I threw a glance at the tools Kresstan was holding, trying very hard to keep calm.

The guards looked at us suspiciously.

"We are delivering these tools to Miss Ella for her ingenious gadgets featuring at the Founding Fest Celebrations," Augusta casually produced the lie as Zella had instructed. "We need to get back into the City to finish our job before the day is over."

"Ah, Miss Ella! I'm a fan of her gadgets!" The guard then turn his attention to Kresstan. "And the Kreepton?"

"He picked out the tools for us." Augusta gestured cheekily at Kresstan. She was quite good at playing her part. "We needed him for the technical parts. Nothing beats the clever little minds of the Kreeptons, right?"

"They are clever alright," the guard said with despise. "Watch your backs! I don't trust these creatures! Lost a good brother of mine to them."

"Absolutely," I responded with sympathy.

The guards waved us through but never took their eyes off of Kresstan until we were beyond their sight. We didn't exchange a word and kept on walking. A few Human passer bys observed Kresstan curiously and mumbled some comments. We pretended not to notice them and just focused on putting one foot in front of the other, taking deep breaths, and looking as relaxed as possible.

Just to be sure we lost all the nosy glances, we made a few extra turns. At the first abandoned alley way we came by, we removed ourselves from view. Hidden, we were finally able to blow a breath of relieve.

"We are in!" I felt an obligation to voice our accomplishment.

"But we are not safe yet. Don't let your guards down," Augusta reminded. "If everyone is ready, let's keep moving."

Peeking out into the open, we found ourselves astonishingly staring into the busy streets of the City! Humans were everywhere! Men, women, children, dressed in all sorts of colors and styles, were traveling in all sorts of directions. Streets were lined with different stores and shops selling an array of goods. The roads were well-paved with cobblestone. Glow stone lamps dotted the sides of the streets. Minecarts three times larger than the usual ran along a network of rails. They were controlled by a complex red stone system, providing quick transportation for the people and their cargos throughout the Kingdom. The passenger carts were elaborately lined with soft wool covered seats and a foldable roof to keep their passengers shielded from the weather. Technologies and luxuries were abundant everywhere we looked.

"Zella said, head towards the giant statue of the King..." Augusta searched in the distance and quickly found the back of a sculpture so large that you could see it throughout the City. "...and you can't miss it..."

Using that massive sculpture as a reference point, we navigated our ways through the city. We passed through a quiet street that looked like a residential area full of multi-story buildings constructed with materials hard to come by.

"A building of quartz and one of Nether bricks!" Remembering how difficult it was to come by all those materials we used, I couldn't imagine how hard the Tallects must have worked to help create this city. "How can one city have this much richness? How much exploiting did the Tyrant do to obtain all these?"

Although Kresstan had been quiet the entire time, I could see that he was a green volcano on the verge of eruption.

After the next turn at the base of the statue, we arrived at a commercial district. According to Zella's instruction, her contact's shop was around here.

The presence of Tallects was hard to miss here. A nervous Skelee was presenting his products to a Human shopkeeper outside a jewelry shop under the supervision of two mean-looking soldiers. Across the street, a Zombie was being yelled at for dropping his tools.

"This is outrageous!" Kresstan erupted. "Those Humans have no respect for the Tallects! I...I..."

"Let it go, Kresstan!" Augusta and I had to restrain Kresstan so he would not rush in to rescue his former citizens. "We are not in the position to help them."

Our little scene certainly did not go unnoticed. "Is that Kreepton causing trouble?" A soldier stopped by to checked out the commotion.

"Oh, no, no. He got worry about not being able to finish his work in time," Augusta made up another excuse. "We'll be taking him back to the shop so he can get back to work. Thanks for asking."

The soldier moved on and we hurried up to dissolve ourselves into the busy street, though it was hard to stay invisible when you have a Kreepton in a city of Humans.

"My apologies, I was carried away." Kresstan got a hold of himself again.

"No worries," I said as we moved quickly down the street. "Let's focus on getting to the shop before we raise any more suspicion."

"There it is!" Augusta spotted our refuge. "Ella's Shop of Gadgets."

The shop seemed to be even smaller than our house back in Tallect, and the store front rather empty. A handful of item frames displaying some odd-looking machines were hanging on the walls. The only piece of furniture in the shop was a three-block-wide counter. A few notebooks and pens scattered on top of it. A girl who looked like she hadn't groom herself in days sat at the counter, busy writing in one of the notebooks in front of her.

"Oh, hello, soldiers, how can I help you?" the girl greeted us as we approached. She wore thick magnifying glasses and a dirty brown lab coat with six pockets full of paper, pens, and tools.

"Are you, by any chance, Ella?" I asked with caution. "We are delivering the Kreepton you requested."

"I am Ella, but I don't recall requesting a Kreepton..." she wondered as I handed her a package with the wooden talisman Zella gave us peeping on the side. Ella swiftly covered it with one of the notebooks, making sure no one else saw it. "Oh! I guess I did!

Please come in for your assignment."

Ella led us behind the counter, through a door, into the back room of the store. The back room was quite a contrast to the uncluttered store front—strange looking gadgets scattered all over the floor, a few chests occupied the corners, drawings of even stranger looking designs were all over the walls, a table in the middle of the room was completely buried under stacks of paper and books.

We struggled to find footing on a floor that didn't really exist. Judging from her looks and the mess, we were a bit reluctant to believe she could be of help. Ella could tell our hesitation.

"I apologize for the mess, I've been busy thinking, no time for cleaning," Ella said as she closed the door of this windowless room. "It may not seem like much here, but I assure you, I have many excellent inventions that were greatly appreciated by the people of Geb."

"Zella trusts that you'll be able to help us," Augusta said. "Guess we are in your capable hands now."

We wasted no time in explaining our situation and that we had to get into the Kreepton Settlement in hopes of learning the secrets of King Steve.

"Fascinating! It's an honor to meet a Kreepton so brave!" Ella shook Kresstan's hand like he was her hero. "How's Zella doing?"

"She's doing fine..." With the Tallects' future at stake, Kresstan was feeling uneasy working with an odd ball like Ella. He uncomfortably retrieved his hand. "How did you come to be...on our side?"

"I understand your suspicion. I am an inventor and I have worked extensively with Kreeptons for my creations. So, I had the chance to get to know them quite well," Ella said as she pushed all the clutter on the table to the floor, leaving just a piece of paper. She got busy drawing out a simple area layout. "Let's just say I don't approve the King's policies towards the Tallects."

"This layout..." Kresstan studied the plan she drew. "Is this the area of the Kreepton Settlement?"

"Precisely." Ella drew a few more marks on the layout. "I am the perfect person to get you in! All the times I've been there to fetch Kreeptons, I know my way around that place like the back of my hand."

Zella did send us to the right help.

"So, how about Beyond the Northern Gate? Do you have any idea what's there?" I asked.

"Don't have the slightest clue," Ella replied as she continued working on the layout. "That place is constantly surrounded by thick fog. The Witches made sure no one can look into what twisted project they are working on."

"A secret even from the Humans..." Kresstan thought deeply.

"Except those most trusted by the King and his Council," Ella clarified. "If information leaked, the pool of suspects would be quite small, so no one would dare to talk."

"The Council... Those Witches..." Kresstan mumbled in frustration under his breath.

"There, it's done," Ella finished her drawing and laid it in the center for all to see. "The Kreepton Settlement sits in the center of Geb's Garrison, across from the King's Castle. It's wrapped securely by the soldier's living quarters and their training ground. Four guard towers on each corner of the Garrison watch over the area. The Settlement itself is enclosed by eight-block-tall stone walls with like a hundred torches all around it, and is patrolled day and night. Anyone who managed to escape those walls would surely be seen under all that light.

There is only one small two block wide iron door that connects the Settlement to the outside. The whole place is like a prison with only one way in and out. Furthermore, the in and out of the Kreeptons are carefully recorded on the log book by the guards on duty."

"How can we possibly get in?" I surveyed the layout, trying to find somewhere to sneak in without being seen.

"Well, a simple distraction would do the trick." Ella giggled mischievously.

Ella pulled out a few mechanical parts under her work table and assembled them into a shooting device with a funnel shaped barrel. "This is a stone vaporizing cannon, still experimental, but I think it'll have great applications."

"Vaporizing!?" I was shocked at the intensity of this 'sneak in' mission. "We are not blowing a hole on the Settlement wall, are we?"

"Of cause not, silly!" Ella laughed. "We just need to blow up enough to create a scene."

"Though I admit I do have a strong desire to bring down the wall," said Kresstan.

"That time will come, my brave Kreepton." Ella gave Kresstan a pat on the shoulder. "Ready to make some trouble?"

Chapter 8:

The Scene at the Settlement

Late afternoon that day, we launched towards the Garrison. Ella led the way wearing an angry face, holding the vaporizer, and stomping all the way to the Garrison just like we rehearsed. We could see King Steve's magnificent Castle sitting on a hill just behind the Garrison. The Tyrant sure kept his most useful servants close to him.

The sound of soldiers training in the Garrison could be heard blocks away, and it got louder as we got closer. I suddenly had a feeling of "home," like it triggered feelings from my childhood.

I gave Augusta a did-you-hear-that look. And she replied me with that I-see-what-you-mean expression. Before we could communicate any further, we were at the Garrison.

We kept our heads down while Ella marched into the Garrison like she owned the place. The soldiers there were not alarmed when they noticed it was her.

We arrived in front of the Settlement in the center with ease. Ella walked up to one of the guards at the Settlement doorway and spilled out her demands.

"THIS IS A JOKE!" she screamed at the guard a hand from his face, gesturing to Kresstan. "I need a more competent Kreepton than this moron!"

"Miss Ella!" What's the issue here?" The guard was taken aback by her aggression. "Let me check the records..."

"Forget the record!" Ella grabbed the log book from the guard and threw it on the floor. "I need another Kreepton assistant so I can finish my project before the big celebration! Better this doesn't go on any record so the King wouldn't find out about this embarrassment on *your* part!"

"I understand. But the record..." The guard kept his cool and bent down to pick up the record book.

"Oh! The King is not going to be waiting if this is not fixed quickly..." Ella swung the vaporizer furiously pointing at a nearby guard tower. Just then, a wave of glowing blue energy discharged from the vaporizer into the middle of the guard tower...

SWOOSH!
PAM!
SWOOSH!!

A good twenty blocks vaporized from the guard tower, sending a few soldiers falling to the ground.

"Blockarama!" The guards froze in place. "What have you done, Miss Ella!"

"Ops..." Ella shrugged with sweet innocence. "That is exactly why I needed this fix... Well, don't just stand there! Let's go help your fellow soldiers."

Pulling the guards with her, Ella headed towards the injured soldiers. The record book was dropped on the floor as they ran towards the collapsed tower. She turned back to us to give us a wink as a cue for us to act our part.

"Right! We'll just take this Kreepton in and keep them in their places." I hustled Augusta and Kresstan through the Settlement iron doors and quickly closed it behind us.

"Good luck, Ella," I looked back and whispered to myself.

I turned around to face the inside of the Settlement. We were surrounded by some twenty Kreeptons looking a bit confused and unfriendly.

"Humans! Is this a treat from Miss Ella?" one Kreepton said. "You dare come in here so outnumbered!"

The Kreeptons forced us away from the door. We backed into a corner deeper into the Settlement.

"My fellow Kreeptons!" Kresstan came between us and the advancing Kreeptons. "I am the once Prince Kresstan! These two Humans helped me journey from our Tallect world all the way here to you. Please do not harm them!"

"You can't be Prince Kresstan! He was killed in the Wars!" Another Kreepton claimed. "The Tyrant's men bought back his sword. For all I know, you could be an impostor!"

"You were deceived!" Kresstan defended. "I lost that sword while fighting the Master Hunters."

"If you are who you claimed to be, then show me the true sword of the royal Prince." A gentle Kreepton lady stepped forward from the crowd.

"Lady Kassandra!" Kresstan recognized the Kreepton and his face lighted up in joy. "There's not a chance I would lose *that* sword!"

Kresstan pulled up his right sleeve to reveal a sword-shaped scar that ran from the back of his hand to his elbow.

"He is indeed, our Prince!" Lady Kassandra declared with delight. "It is a scar left by an experiment he and I conducted when we were young Kreeps."

The crowd of Kreeptons cheered. They were overjoyed to have their Prince in their mist. Kresstan instantly regained that long-lost confidence to lead his kind. He, once again, saw a future for them.

But celebration was short lived, Kresstan bought their attention to our more pressing matter.

"As much as I would like to hear everything of your encounters after the Wars, we have very little time here. I must first request your help," Kresstan addressed the crowd with his royal authority, "I have reasons to believe if we could learn of the Tyrant's secret Beyond the Northern Gate, we may have a chance to fight back and regain our freedom."

"Any chance to take back Tallect!" the crowd cheered.

Lady Kassandra quieted the crowd. "I know a thing or two about the Northern Gate," she said. "My father is the lead scientist working directly on the project beyond the Gate, and we've been trying to work out a way to get in there. But first, we need to get your Human friends out of here. The guards would become alarmed if they don't get out soon."

"That's right, we don't want Ella to get into more trouble," Augusta said. "But can you really do anything without help from Humans?"

"There is a plan we've been fashioning for a while. Given that no one else knows our Prince is in Geb, I think you may be able to pull it off," Lady Kassandra proposed after some thoughts. "The Founding Fest will be held two days from now to celebrate the founding of Geb. Extra help will be needed in the Castle. We will arrange Prince Kresstan to be sent to the Castle as help, while you can have Ella arrange you two as Human helpers. You can meet up in the Castle to put our plan into action."

Kassandra pulled out a piece of paper and jotted down "D2 St22" and handed it to us. "Give this to Ella and she'll know where to direct you."

After wishing the Kreeptons good luck, we exited the Settlement, taking great care not to look like we were involved in a secret scheme.

Ella just finished helping the soldiers to repair the vaporized guard tower. We picked up the log book on the floor and chose a spot to quickly forge Ella's request for a Kreepton.

"Everything is good as new, right, officers?" Ella said with satisfaction.

The soldiers shot Ella a look of annoyance as we approached them.

"Miss Ella, the Kreepton has been returned," I informed our collaborator. "Are you *sure* you need another one of those headaches?"

Catching my hint, Ella conveniently mustered an artificial sense of guilt towards the mess. "You know what? Save your troubles, forget about a Kreepton! I'll just finish the project myself."

"Ms. Ella here won't be causing any more problems." Augusta handed the guard the log book, "I have marked in here that the Kreepton she requested has been returned. We'll just escort her back to her shop so you may all return to your duties."

"Thank you, soldiers." The guard took the log book but his eyes lingered on our faces. "You two don't look familiar..."

"Oh, we are new recruits," Augusta quickly said with a smile. "That's why we get jobs like dealing with Ms. Ella."

The guard chuckled and waved us away.

"That was a bold move!" I said to Ella when we were out of the earshot of the guard. "Aren't you worried they would arrest you?"

"Hey, you guys improvised very well." Ella gave me a pat on the back. "They wouldn't dare arresting the daughter of a Councilman!"

"Councilman!?" Augusta said with reserve. "That explained why you are so fearless."

"I know what you are thinking." Ella saw our unease. "Why would a Councilman's daughter help the Tallects?"

"Yes, why?" I asked.

"Well, you can say I'm not the obedient type!" Ella laugh. "I simply do what I think is right."

We headed back to Ella's shop. Inside the safety of the back room, we updated her on the plan to meet Kresstan in the Castle during the Founding Fest, and handed her the piece of paper from Kassandra.

"Brilliant!" Ella exclaimed and got lost in her own thoughts. "D2 St22 and the Founding Fest! The perfect cover!"

"Do share the good news, Ms. Ella," said Augusta.

"We kept hearing about this Founding Fest, what happens in that anyway?" I asked.

"Ah, the Founding Fest. Every one hundred days, the citizens of Geb commemorate the founding of our Kingdom with a grand celebration." Ella informed us. "In the morning, the King will give a speech at the market square in front of the Castle, follow by a few performances and a big feast for the people in the Castle. And finally, a spectacular firework display will conclude the day's events. The Kingdom's latest inventions will also be exhibited on that day. That's when my stone vaporizer will have its debut!"

"What a day!" Augusta said.

"And that stone vaporizer..." I couldn't help but to find amusement remembering the scene at the

Settlement. "It would be quite a spectacle itself! Ha ha..."

"I made a fool out of myself, didn't I?" Ella crossed her arms in protest.

"It's all for a good cause," Augusta reassured Ella.

Ella smiled proudly in response.

"So how is this Fest going to help us?" I asked.

"Right. It's the one day when everyone participates and keeps pretty busy," Ella continued excitingly. "A perfect time to sneak around the Castle!"

"Excellent!" Augusta shared Ella's enthusiasm.

"And this D2 St22?" I pointed to the piece of paper.

"As for that..." Ella pulled out a complex-looking floorplan from under her work table.

"This is the floorplan of the King's Castle," Ella introduced. "It's consisted of two main buildings—the Work Building and the Castle itself. The preparations for the Fest will be held in the Work Building mostly. Then people will gather in the Reception Hall on the first floor of the Castle for the feast. Nearly the whole of Geb will be there."

"Sounds like crazily crowded!" Augusta thought. "A perfect way to hide in plain sight."

"It's a fest after all," Ella agreed. She directed our attention to the area marked "Dungeon." "'D2 St22' is a storage room in the dungeon underneath the Work Building."

She ran her hand over a series of rooms identical in size laid out on the floorplan and stopped on one of them. She then marked the room with a red pen and drew a line indicating the route to get there from an area marked "Kitchen."

"There's a trap door in the kitchen that will take you down to the dungeon." "'D2' is the second level of the Dungeons, 'St22' is storage room 22. Everyone is required to listen to the King's speech. The whole storage area will be pretty abandoned at that time. Take this route during the speech and there's little chance that you'll be seen."

"An ideal place to meet up!" I said.

"Joining the Fest is one thing, but in order to get to 'D2 St22,' you need a special identity. Extra helpers are hired to help with the preparations. Helpers will be gathering at the Work Building and then send to work in different areas. Hmm...And you'll need to get into the kitchen. I think I can get you to work there."

"The kitchen, of all places!" I grumbled. "Cooking is not exactly my forte...My favorite food to cook would be food that are already cooked!"

"Don't mind him, Ella," Augusta laughed. "He's just kidding."

"Ha! Very funny!" Ella laughed sarcastically and ignored me.

And so our plan was designed.

After setting us up with food and beds in the back room of her shop, Ella left us to make some arrangements for our disguises.

We spent the next day memorizing the floorplan to best fool-proved our venturing into the Castle. Not knowing what Lady Kassandra was planning to have us do in the Castle, it was extra important that we knew the Castle inside and out.

The Castle had five floors, the first floor was the Reception Hall, the middle three floors were rooms for the residents of the Castle, and the top floor was the Grand Hall and the King's Private Chamber. In addition, there was an underground prison and two towers on each side at the back.

The traffic outside Ella's shop increased as the Fest

drew near. People were dressing up the streets with all kinds of banners, as well as dressing themselves up in fancy styles for the occasion. Hidden by the festive atmosphere, Augusta and I waited quietly for the moment to make our move.

Chapter 9:
D2 St22

In the early morning of the Founding Fest Day, Ella showed up with some identification papers and two orange vests for us to put on. After a few words of cautions, Ella sent us on our way while she stayed to make some finishing touches on her vaporizer for the invention exhibits.

Taking the same route toward the Garrison, this time, we passed it and arrived at the Castle Complex behind it. Wearing our vests, we blended in with other people uniformly wearing orange in front of the Work Building. A bored-looking officer sat behind a table, routinely checked the identification papers of the helpers. One by one, he directed everyone in line to their place of work.

As we waited, we took mental notes of our surroundings, matching them to the floorplans we studied.

The mixed red bricks and wood Work Building was

a good ten blocks tall, but it was still dwarfed by the neighboring Castle. The Castle functioned as the King and the Council's offices and residences. Up close, this grand construction was even more amazing. Color-changing pale blue green prismarine, a rare ocean material, adorned the outer walls, creating an illusion like the Castle was made of ocean water. Stained sandstone steps accented the walls in a stylish arrangement to give it an elegant texture. Colorful banners of various designs served as decoration. Solid gold blocks were used to make the four-by-four double door entrance.

And that feeling of familiarity crossed my mind again! The color scheme somehow triggered a memory of some sort... Like a déjà vu.

The line moved quicker than expected while we admired the view.

"NEXT!" the bored-looking officer called us. It was our turn.

We handed those papers Ella prepared to the officer. It claimed that we were excellent cooks and were recommended by Councilman Quebo's household with a seal of approval.

"You will be working in the kitchen preparing food for the feast," the officer said plainly after he bought into those lies on the paper. He roughly pinned a card with a big "K" on our vests. "Head to the Work Building and someone will point you to the right place. NEXT!"

Augusta and I moved promptly to make way for the next person and approached the Work Building.

Standing on the right side of the Castle, the Work Building housed the servants' quarter, crafting room, and the kitchen. A number of servants' corridors connected the Work Building to the Castle, allowing servants to attend to the residents of the Castle.

The click we stepped inside the Building, it was like entering a hectic bee hive—workers in orange were swarming in all sorts of directions, carrying out their tasks. We were stunned at the entrance, trying to figure out our next step.

An impatient man wearing a long dark blue leather robe barked out orders to the workers that came in. "Kitchen is back there!" Noticing the "K" on our vest, he pointed us to a door at the back wall.

We played a good game of "dodging the orange bees" and successfully arrived in the kitchen.

"You! Newbies!" A cook spotted us as soon as we stepped through the kitchen door. "Go bake those potatoes over there! And hurry!"

We looked to the direction the cook was pointing at, and spotted a few mounts of potatoes taller than us sitting next to towers of furnaces.

"OK... Let's keep up our appearance..." I said to Augusta with a painful grin.

The morning wore on, and the smoke in the kitchen was sickening. A thousand cooked potatoes later, our chance to escape this tedious work finally came. In readying for the feast, the kitchen workers started to move the cooked food to the Reception Hall in the Castle through a connecting hallway.

"The King is about to give his speech!" someone announced around midday. "Finish what you are doing and gather in front of the Castle!"

"That's our cue," I whispered to Augusta, hinting at those workers heading out of the kitchen.

"About time we are done with these potatoes," Augusta sighed with relief. "I don't think I'll be eating potatoes for some moon cycles to come!"

Following the other workers, we took an inventory full of potatoes to the Reception Hall on the first floor of the Castle. We laid them out neatly on the long table placed in the middle of the Hall. But instead of returning to the kitchen to get more potatoes, on our way back, we tucked ourselves behind some stacks of chests when nobody was looking. We found that trap door Ella had marked on the floorplans and down we went.

Below the trap door was cramped and dark. Few torches lighted the way in the tunnel walkway of only two blocks wide and two blocks tall. Rows of storage room doors lined the walkway left and right. Each door was marked with its designated number. The first one on our right read "D1 St1".

To use the space most efficiently, the storage rooms' arrangement created many intersections that looked just the same as one another. It could easily confuse anyone's orientation. Lucky for us, we had the floorplan in our heads to guide us. We easily found the next trap door that descended us even deeper underground into Dungeon level two.

More doors marked and arranged the same way as the first level.

... "D2 St18"... "D2 St19"... "D2 St20"... "D2 St21"...

At last, we arrived at a door marked "D2 St22."

I nervously pushed open the door to this storage not knowing what I would find in there. Then, a tremendous sense of joy came over us at the sight of Kresstan waiting for us behind that door!

"Aren't we glad to see you!" Augusta gave Kresstan a big hug. "It was the longest day and a half without you!"

"The feeling is mutual, my friends." Kresstan returned the embrace but quickly moved on to give us an update on his findings. "I have received the information we seek from Lady Kassandra."

"Do share!" I said.

"King Steve indeed hid his power over the worlds Beyond the Northern Gate," he told us with a serious frown. "The last time Kassandra heard from her father, they were working on multiple Obelisk portals."

"Multiple Obelisks!?"

"Research shows that different building materials can link different worlds together. Like sandstones links Tallect to Geb, other materials could link Geb to other worlds." Kresstan explained. "Seems like the Tyrant is not satisfied with just Tallect!"

"So there are other worlds out there?" I wondered.

"That seems to be the theory," Kresstan continued. "Only members of his trusted Council are allowed in on the details. Even Ella, daughter of a Councilman does not know the full extent of the research."

"That sounds like trouble..." I said.

"I certainly do not wish the horror of Tallect bestow upon another civilization." Kresstan crunched his fist tightly.

"So, what's the plan?" Augusta asked.

"Destroy everything beyond the Gate," Kresstan said firmly.

"That won't stop the Tyrant from rebuilding them again..." I said.

"But it'll create chaos, at least temporarily. Then maybe it'll give the Tallects the chance to escape the City. We can then regroup and find a way to defeat the King," Kresstan continued dimly. "Certainly, it's no easy task. The Gate is made of obsidian and guards protect the area at all times. If we somehow got past the guards, we'd still need an obsidian key to unlock the Gate. Such a key is believed to be hidden somewhere in the King's

Private Chamber."

"So, the first step is to find that key?" Augusta asked.

"Precisely!" Kresstan confirmed.

"Even if we find the key, wouldn't the King notice if it's missing?" I asked.

"That's why Lady Kassandra gave me this decoy." Kresstan pulled out a purplish black key from his overcoat pocket. "Her father forged it when they came up with the idea to destroy the Obelisks."

"So, how are we better at carrying out this idea?" Augusta asked.

"Because hardly anyone knows we are here, we are invisible to the King and much of Geb. The decoy should buy us some time from the unsuspecting King, enough for us to find a way to get through the Gate and destroy everything."

"Now, if the scientists knew that much, what's keeping them from betraying the King and destroying everything there themselves?" I wondered.

"TNTs," said Kresstan. "The Settlement is surrounded by explosives. If the Kreeptons didn't perform as asked, with a simple order from the Castle, the Settlement would be blown to pieces."

"That is one dirty trick!" The idea upset Augusta.

"Including myself, there are only twenty-eight Kreeptons left," Kresstan added. "As long as there's hope that we would be free one day and rebuild our society, we would do anything we must to survive."

"That means we also have to disable the TNTs before we blow anything up," Augusta thought out loud. "All these are going to take some extensive planning."

"Correct..." Kresstan acknowledged the difficulty in this monumental task.

"Risky, but at this point, it's all or nothing," said

Augusta.

"Let's not waste time then!" I said as I reached for the door. "Let's get that key and we'll go from there!"

"Wait! You'll need these, "Kresstan took out two sets of armors and swords. "No Kreepton walking around without escorts."

"Where did you get that?" Augusta and I put the armors on.

"My previous escorts..." Kresstan chuckled, flexing his arm. "I left them in one of the storage rooms to take a nap."

With high spirits and the confidence that we could somehow save the Tallects, we left "D2 St22" and back into the dim tunnels.

Our next stop: The King's Chamber.

Chapter 10:
What Waited on the Top Floor

Little was known about the King's Chamber. Only the King and the Witches were allowed in there. Rumor said that it was the most protected place in Geb. The Chamber had a separate layer of wall and is only connected to the rest of the Castle through a doorway at the back of the Grand Hall. It would be quite the challenge just to get in there.

Even with that said, we did not have a whole lot of

time to be overly cautious. We had to climb out of the storage dungeon, pass through the servants' corridors, and hike up the stairs all the way to the fifth floor of the Castle UNDETECTED. Then, we had to figure out how to get inside the Chamber, and last but not least, sneak back down to the first floor and escape the Castle with the key.

All these had to be done before the feast was over. We sure hoped the King would stay downstairs and enjoy the celebrations till the end.

I took the lead and proceeded down the tunnel to get back above ground. The course of action was clear, but there was still something troubling me.

"I know I'm repeating myself, but I need to get it off my chest." I stopped Kresstan on his path. "I need to know if you can still trust us."

"Sure I do." Kresstan said firmly. "For all that you have done, how could I not?"

"But I'm afraid we've been having this strange feeling since we arrived in Geb," said Augusta. "It feels like we've been here before, but we can't recall a thing. We don't even know ourselves anymore. For all I know, we may be on Geb's side."

"If you were, you aren't anymore." Kresstan looked at us kindly. "If you had ever done any wrong to the Tallects, you must had been deceived and tricked to do the Tyrant's biddings."

"Thanks for believing in us," Augusta was glad to hear that.

We found our way to yet another trap door that would take us directly underneath the Castle, and into the servants' corridors. We stealthily climbed the ladder up to the trap door, taking great caution to not make any sound unnecessary.

"Clear," I whispered, peeking out from the trap door.

We climbed out of the opening quietly and exited the dungeon into a long narrow hallway of only three blocks wide. A series of staircases at the end of the hallway extended upwards all the way to the top of the Castle.

The staircases in the servants' corridor was our express ticket to the Grand Hall.

"The Castle seems rather deserted," Kresstan observed as we climbed up the staircase. "Even with the celebrations happening outside, a royal castle should not be this quiet."

"Could this be a trap?" I thought.

"But who else knows we are here?" said Augusta.

"In any case, it is too late to turn back now." Kresstan kept moving up.

We reached the top floor without seeing as little as a servant.

From the corridor, a chiseled quartz arch doorway opened into the Grand Hall. The Grand Hall was a large space with a dimension of about twenty by twenty-five blocks and a five-block-high ceiling, but it was barely lit with only a hand full of torches. Quartz pillars surrounded the Hall. We used the pillars to conceal ourselves in the dark. A long table with twenty or so cushioned chairs was placed in the middle. This was likely the place where the King's Council created those criminal policies against the Tallects. At the back was a pair of large arch doors lavishly decorated with emeralds, diamonds, and glow stone dust.

"That must be the Chamber." I pointed to the jeweled entrance.

"I have a bad feeling about this," said Augusta. "It's

all too easy."

"Well, we won't get a chance like this again." I searched in the dark for the handle to open the arch doors.

Just when we thought we were close to finding the obsidian key, the arch doors opened itself. Followed by the appearance of a dark figure, with a face we had seen on that giant statue...A deep voice sounded from it.

"Ah, took you long enough to get here."

"King Steve!" Our shocks were in unison.

King Steve approached us calmly and with overwhelming authorities, forcing us to back away from the arch doors. He was well protected by a full set of diamond armor. A ruby adored his chest plate. The gold crown on his head was crafted with so many details that it could only be the work of a skilled Skelee goldsmith. With the raise of his arm, the Grand Hall was lighted up, unveiling all the glory in the splendid space. Soldiers in full armors emerged from all sides of the Hall, surrounding us.

We responsively pulled out our swords in defense.

"Do not harm them," King Steve commended as he took a closer look at Kresstan. "That crest on your coat...If I may take a guess, do I have the honor of finally meeting Prince Kresstan of the Kreeptons?"

"As unwilling as I am to give you that honor, I am, indeed, the Prince you have failed again and again to capture," Kresstan mocked the King.

"And yet, here you are. Delivered to me at last," King Steve returned the mocking, "succumbed to my tricks."

"So, this *is* a trap after all!" Kresstan was angry at himself for not being able to outwit the King.

"Do you really think a Kreepton could wonder free

in my Kingdom without proper authority given by my Council?" King Steve had great confidence in the security of his territory. "My men had reported two unreasonably fearless soldiers entering the Kreepton Settlement and coming out unharmed. No Human is safe with those savages unless he is scheming with those Tallects. So, I decided to wait and see what you were up to."

"Who is the savage? Even your own people defy your tyranny!" Kresstan challenged.

"Do they?" King Steve laughed triumphantly. "It took some efforts, but Hadrian and Augusta did such an excellent job of bringing you to me."

Kresstan stared at us in disbelieve.

"He knows you by name...? You serve the King?" Kresstan was so petrified that he couldn't even say another word. All he managed to do was to step away from us.

"No! Kresstan! We are not working for him!" I yelled in defense. "You said you trust us!"

"While yes, those two are members of my elite Master Hunters," King Steve confirmed Kresstan's suspicion. "I sent so many mobs into Tallect for the Wars that it became rather difficult to mine there. They are those Hunters I sent to get rid of the mobs and also any Tallects that survived. Why else would you think they worked so hard to bring you here to me, Prince?"

"That can't be true!" I was furious, how could he frame us as his agents. "Augusta and I can't be part of this Hunter deal!"

"How did I not see that...?" Augusta was mumbling in a low voice, losing in her own thoughts, trying to remember. "All that fighting against the mobs... was what we were meant to do..."

"It seems your memories have been affected, but I believe we can have that fixed. You'll be well taken care of for your great work. Anything for my loyal subjects!" The King laughed and signaled his soldiers. "You, Prince, on the other hand, I have other plans for you. Take him away. I have a festival to return to."

Before King Steve left the Grand Hall, he threw Kresstan one last blow. "Oh, by the way, Prince, that lady Kreepton will be joining you shortly."

Kresstan had defeat written all over him. Not only did he failed the Tallects, he even failed to protect his childhood friend, Lady Kassandra.

The soldiers approached Kresstan with their swords drawn.

"Don't touch him!" I yelled and waved my sword at the soldiers.

"Hadrian! Don't even bother!" Kresstan dropped his sword and lifted his hands up in surrender. "I'm no longer your business."

"Kresstan! You can't believe we lied to you!" I protested.

"I don't know what to believe anymore. I lost this fight. I am not worthy of my rank." Kresstan went limp.

A handful of soldiers restrained Kresstan by the arms and took him away. Leaving Augusta and me with a dozen other armed soldiers.

Chapter 11:
The Master Hunters

The soldiers ceased our weapons and armors and chained our hands behind our backs. Then we were pushed out of the Grand Hall by two soldiers. Our minds were too confused and scattered to even put up a fight. They took Augusta and me through a small door off to one side of the Hall and up a narrow spiral staircase. We realized we were going up one of the towers of the Castle, and soon, the stairs ran out. An old dark oak door stood between us and the horror behind.

"Madam Wicka." One of the soldiers knocked on the door. "The King asked for your service."

"Ah, the scatterbrained Hunters I heard. "A high pitch voice screeched from behind the door. "Bring them in!"

As soon as the door opened, a suffocating smell of death rushed into our noses. It smelled like fermented spider eyes wrapped in rotten pork chop infected with green slimy mold! Not that I knew what that smelled like, but I believed that described the stench about right.

The owner of that high pitch voice was sitting in one of the two chairs next to a table full of brewing stands. She wore a black pointy hat ornate with an emerald and a long purple robe that indicated that she could only be one of those vicious creatures that sold out the Tallects—a Witch!

The room we entered was small and dim without a single window except for a tiny skylight glass on its pyramid-shaped ceiling. Its walls were lined with shelves packed with books and bottles containing various colors of liquid and powder.

"The King mentioned they have some memory lost?" Wicka the Witch picked up a magnifying glass with a lens that gleamed in an eerie purple color like the glow of a Nether Portal. She examined Augusta and me through the glass. "But before I restore those memories, looks like I have quite a lot of orbs to extract."

"Extract!?" We were alarmed by the sound of that. "What orbs?"

"The life force orbs, also called the XP orbs. The King is collecting them for his grand project," Wicka explained as she checked on the slimy green goo brewing at the brewing stand. "Whenever you kill something, you received their life force, it's how the worlds recycle energy. Normally the energy stays in you till it's your turn to die, but I've found a way to extract them while you are still alive."

"This amount should be safe to keep you two alive." She poured out two small cups of the green goo and shoved it to our faces. "Drink this and it'll be over before you know it."

We stared at that foul-smelling goo and already wanted to throw up, let alone putting that to our mouths! But the soldiers behind us prevented us from backing away from it.

"Come on! Do we need to do this the hard way?" Wicka grumbled. She waved to the soldiers, "We've got a lot to do!"

"Yes, ma'am." The soldiers took the cups, jammed them to our mouths, and forced us to swallow it. I felt that goo ran down my throat like hot lava. It burned so bad that I felt like my insides were going to spill out of me.

And it did!

Within moments, waves of colorful glowing orbs rushed out of our mouths. It felt like I was being gutted! Augusta and I let out a cry in pain. Our voices echoed in the small room...

Wicka opened an enchanted diamond chest to collect the orbs that came out of us. That was the last thing I saw before I fainted...

∞ଫଫଫଫଫଫଫଫଫଫଫ∞

I woke up to a chain of explosions. When I opened my eyes, I saw colorful lights shining through that small skylight in Wicka's room. I was still stuck in there!

"Ah! Took you long enough to wake up. The fireworks for the celebration already started," Wicka's voice scratched near my ear. "I was already done with your friend."

"Augusta! What did you do to her?" I sat up quickly, but my light headedness forced me to drop right back down.

"Easy there!" Wicka went behind me and forced my head onto a block. "I finished the enchantment on her and she's now resting in the guest room."

"Enchantment?"

Then, I noticed the diamonds at the corners of the block I was laying on, and my "pillow" was, actually, a book. I was on an enchantment table!

"You can't enchant my head!" I tried to break free from Wicka's hold.

"Not your head! Just your memory." Wicka tightened her grip. "Cooperate or you'll get hurt if I'm interrupted."

Before I could protest any more, Wicka started the enchantment. The firework outside continued but the explosions started to sound more and more distant, and the color turned into a swirl... Everything went white, I entered a dream-like state...

∞⋈⋈⋈⋈⋈⋈⋈⋈⋈⋈⋈⋈∞

When my vision began to clear, I was in a jungle biome with Augusta and a team of King Steve's Hunters. We stood next to a lake, and I could see my reflection in the water. I was carrying an enchanted sword and bow, and wearing a full set of black iron armor.

A crest was on the collar of the chest plate. Its fine details depicted a crown slipped over an upright sword. Twelve small swords radiating out from the center. I recognized this crest from a banner on the wall of the Castle. The design represented the twelve Master Hunters as protectors of the King.

How proud I was to be wearing that black armor! I was ready to take on any enemy.

Something moved in the bushes just twenty blocks away. Our fellow Hunters were ready to attack. A group of armed and fierce Kreeptons jumped out, rushed towards us with the intention to kill...

"NOOO!" I came back to the present and awoke on a bed.

Was that a dream?

"Hadrian!" Augusta stood next to me. I was no longer in the Witch's "chamber of horror."

"Thank the Lord of the Blocks, you finally woke up!" Her expression showed relief.

"Augusta!" I was so thankful to see her. "Where are we?"

"We are in a guest room on the third floor of the Castle."

I looked around the room. It was a simple room of eight by six, furnished with two beds, a table and two chairs. One of its stone walls was decorated with a painting of King Steve standing majestically as ruler of the Kingdom. A window next to the beds looked out to a steep drop to the ground below.

"We are still alive. I guess the King decided to forgive us," Augusta said.

"I had a terrible dream that we were King Steve's Hunters!"

"I don't think that was a dream..." Augusta spoke carefully. "I think Wicka really did restored our memories."

"No! I don't believe that!" I wanted to find a reason to believe otherwise. "If it were really my memories, how come I only 'remember' a random fragment?"

"Wicka said it takes some time for the enchantment to fully work. Our memories will come back piece by piece till they are fully restored."

"Is it a memory enchantment or brainwashing trick?" I rejected Augusta's explanation. "And why are you speaking for that crazy Witch? Are you on her side now? On the Tyrant's side? I have to get out of here!"

I pushed Augusta aside and headed for the door, but she quickly tackled me and pinned me to the floor, face down!

Ouch!

The talisman Zella gave us shot out of my pocket and flew across the room.

"Hadrian! Calm down!" Augusta tried to restrain me. "I know it's hard to believe, but you have to accept who we are!"

"Let go of me!" I shouted, struggling to break free of Augusta's hold.

"Stop it!" Augusta gestured to the door, she got close to my ear and spoked softly. "They are listening."

"Do you need any assistance, Master Augusta?" a man's voice came from behind the door.

"No, I have him under control," Augusta replied. "Thanks for the offer."

She pulled me back up, sat me down on one of the chairs, and picked up the talisman from across the room. She then spoke just loud enough for me to hear.

"First of all, I don't want you to think I've given up on Kresstan and the Tallects," she handed me back the talisman and said with a new found authority. "The enchantment worked quite well on me. I remembered being recruited as a Hunter and pieces of my life here in Geb. "Somehow I know they *are* my memories."

"So which side do you belong to now?" I questioned with suspicion.

"Just because I was a Hunter doesn't mean I can't change," she stated. "I can't agree with our people's treatment of the Tallects after knowing what the King did."

"So we rescue Kresstan?"

"In time, we will," she assured me. "But first, we need to gain back the King's trust."

"I'm in! What's the plan?"

In order to be more believable to the Council, we decided it was best to let our memories come back fully before making any moves. In the next few days, we stayed in our room, ate the food that the servants brought us obediently, and refrained from talking to anyone.

Within the moon cycle, bits by bits, our memories

were fully restored. We were finally able to piece back together our lives.

Augusta and I were orphaned by the Creeper Wars. Our parents served the King as Creeper handlers in Tallect, but they never made it back to Geb alive. We grew up in the same Garrisons that now surrounded the Kreepton Settlements. Our superiors preyed on our bitterness of losing our parents to brainwash us into believing how cruel the Tallects were. We blamed the Tallects for our lost and suffering. As we grew, so did our hatred towards the Tallects.

Although we were devoted soldiers, we were too young to take part in the Creeper Wars. By the time we were properly trained and ready to fight, the Wars were nearly over. The King's Council, instead, enlisted us as Master Hunters—a prestigious rank given to the twelve most loyal and skilled soldiers.

We went to Tallect with a team of Hunters led by Captain Famosa with the hope to avenge our families. During a fight with the surviving Tallects, we lost our footings and fell down a cliff into a fast flowing river.

Our team did not expect us to survive, but we did somehow. Our armors absorbed much of the fall and shattered; our weapons swallowed by the current. When we were washed up near the jungle where we made our house, we had no recollection of who we were nor what we were doing before. That was how our simple lives in Tallect began.

Perhaps it was fate that we met Kresstan. Because of our involvement in his mission, we were able to reclaim our identities. By learning the whole truth, we were given the chance to undo the damages Geb had done to Tallect. And we were determined to make that happen!

To begin, we needed to understand more of the

current situation of Geb. As far as the Council was concern, we were still risks. In order to prevent any trouble we could cause, we were kept locked up in our room until we could prove our loyalty to the King.

Only guards outside our door and servants that brought us food were allowed in. Using our charms and adventure stories, we befriended a few of them. Their gossips provided us some pretty useful information.

"Ella's Gadget Shop was raided," a guard brought us some news. "Captain Famosa led a team to confiscate all of Miss Ella's inventions and notes in hopes to discover other members of the Underground Network."

"So, the Council knows of her involvement with those Tallects?" Augusta asked.

"They sure do now, after she helped you sneak into the Castle!" the guard stated.

"Fabulous!" Augusta pretended to be delighted. "Our mistakes ended up exposing a real traitor!"

"Ha! Some mistakes they were!" the guard joked.

"Did they find anything useful?" I asked.

"As far as I know, other than providing the Captain's team a good afternoon laugh with her crazy ideas, Ella's notes contained nothing about the Network," the guard said.

"What a shame! Wish we knew something useful!" I lied. "I wonder what those Tallects are scheming?"

"Who knows, those Kreeptons in the prison won't spill a thing either," the guard complained.

"You mean the Prince and that lady?" Augusta asked. "They are still alive?"

"They sure are," said the guard. "I heard the King has plans for them."

"Oh! I can't wait to find out what they are!" Augusta acted excitingly.

We urgently needed to figure out what the Council was up to before they could do harm to our Tallect friends. I bet our behaviors were reported, as we had hoped, our opportunity came sooner than expected.

"It's your lucky day, Master Hunters," a messenger from the Council announced to us one afternoon. "The King has requested your presence at dinner tonight!"

That evening, the messenger accompanied us to the Grand Hall. We entered using the beautiful white staircase out in the open, and not the servant's corridor like we did last time we were here. It was an odd feeling being in that place again. Everything about Geb, about the Castle was so familiar and yet so foreign. That anger towards the Tallects we felt as children was no longer there. Instead, we were enraged by the King's deceiving lies.

When we arrived, the entire King's Council was already assembled at the long table. King Steve sat in the middle of the table with the door to his Chamber behind him. Wicka and another older Witch sat on his right and a familiar Master Hunter sat on his left. The other Master Hunters and five more Councilmen filled the remaining seats.

"Ah, the miraculous survivors!" the King greeted us and gestured us to sit at the empty seats across from him, a position of high honor. "Wicka informed me that the memory enchantment should have taken full effect by now. How do you feel?"

"Never better, my King," I said as I sat down. "Glad to be back!"

"I feel foolish to have sided with those Tallects, but our minds are cleared now," Augusta said proudly.

"Excellent," the King said. "I'm sure you remember your fellow Hunters."

"Of course," I said as we nodded to the ten Master Hunters at the table. "It's good to see our brothers in arms again."

They remained silent and returned our nods with cold calculating eyes.

"And also my other Councilmen," the King introduced.

They, too, nodded with indifference.

"It's an honor." Augusta gave a charming smile.

King Steve glanced at our simple and unflattering outfits made of wool and gave a "tsk-tsk" of disapproval. "I'm afraid those clothes of yours are inappropriate for your positions."

He ordered the guards to present to us two sets of black iron armors—uniforms of the Master Hunters, along with a chest of gold, emeralds, and rubies.

"What have we done to deserve such gifts?" Augusta exclaimed.

"You have suffered enough during your exile in Tallect. I'm simply returning what was owed to my loyal subjects," the King said with a gentle smile.

The rest of the Council had rather blank expressions that it was hard to tell of their thoughts on our rewards. Perhaps the King's generosity was nothing new. Such was the way he blinded the people from seeing his cruelty towards the Tallects.

Seeing that there was no point in refusing, we stood up to accept the chest of treasures and suited up in the armors. Our new appearance instantly blended us in with those Master Hunters at the table.

"Now you look much better," the King raised his glass and proposed a toast. "To rewelcome our brave Hunters!"

"To the Hunters," the Council followed the toast in

unison.

"Councilman Quebo," the King called on one of the gentlemen who resembled Ella's features, "the memory enchantment worked wonders, perhaps a reverse one should be casted on your ungracious daughter, so she may forget those Tallects and rejoin her Human family."

"Thank you, my King, I will consider your offer," Councilman Quebo replied with some awkwardness.

"May I ask what happened to that traitor Ella?" Augusta asked the King.

"She's under house arrest in the Castle awaiting trial." The King looked over to Councilman Quebo. "The Council is well aware of the Underground Network. We just did not expect the family of a Councilman could be mixed up in this traitors' network. We hope she would recant her childish sense of justice to save Councilman Quebo some heartache."

"Don't mind that silly girl. We are glad to see you two alive," said the man sitting to the left of the King. His firm but caring voice was all too familiar to us. He was Captain Famosa, the leader of the Master Hunters, the one who led our team of Hunters to Tallect.

The Captain was a small man. But his size did not diminish the intimidation his diamond sword-sharp eyes had on his enemies. He had always been the fatherly figure we looked up to.

"Perhaps the two of you can get the list of the rebels out of her?" the Captain challenged us.

"I like your idea, Captain," the King said. "Prove your worth, Hadrian and Augusta, and I'll have you join my most trusted Council as your brothers in arms did."

"We would be grateful to take on the task," I answered with a bow.

We just signed ourselves up to betray the Tallects.

"I await your result on that." The King then turned to Wicka. "I believe there's also the matter of the Kreeptons."

"Yes, my King," Wicka said with a wickedly delighted grin. "The Prince had been through quite a lot of battles, I'm confident that he would yield over two thousand orbs."

"And I'm afraid our lead scientist had leaked out too much information to his family." King Steve threw down that fake obsidian key from Kassandra in front of us. "As much as I hate to affect his research, that daughter of his has to be set as an example to the Kreeptons who wish to defy our Kingdom."

"I would love to add her to the contribution!" Wicka's excitement was unmistakably twisted. "The lady Kreepton would give us a solid five hundred orbs!"

"That's good news," the old Witch finally spoke with a scratchy low voice. "We'll have enough to enchant the next Obelisk."

Orbs? Obelisk? They are going to extract the orbs out of Kresstan and Kassandra? And enchant an Obelisk?

Our surprise must have shown on our faces, the King turned to us. "Madam Wilcara, would you please fill them in with the fate of their delivery."

"Certainly." The old Witch looked at us with narrowing eyes like a teacher looking at troublemakers. She had reservation on trusting us. "I'm sure you are familiar with the Obelisk, they explode when a teleportation is made. While you were lost in Tallect, we have developed the enchantment to allow it to withstand the energy surge and not be blown to pieces."

"Enchanting a whole Obelisk!" Wicka indulged herself in the idea of it. "It was a beautiful sight the last time we did it!"

"Such an enchantment requires the energy of five thousand orbs," the old Witch continued, ignoring Wicka. "We have been collecting them, and the pair of Kreeptons will provide us with the amount we still need for our second Obelisk."

"So, you'll feed them that nasty green goo you gave us to achieve that?" I winked my nose, remembering that ordeal.

"Oh, yes! I need to make so much of it to extract every last orb out of them!" Wicka could barely contain her cruel eagerness. "I still need a good five days to finish making an inventory of it!"

"Every last one?" Augusta asked. "What would happen to them?"

"Simply put," the King said casually as he raised the glass to have another drink, "life cannot exist without the orbs."

They are going to kill Kresstan and Kassandra! And we have five days to save them!

Chapter 12:
The Scientist and
the Old Witch

The King and his Council brought us up to date on

the development of Geb over that meal, while we sat through reports after reports, pretending very hard to share their pride in our spectacular Kingdom. It felt like hundreds of moon cycles had passed when we were finally dismissed.

We kept up the devoted-Master-Hunter masks all the way back to our room, chatting enthusiastically about the news we just learned. But once we were back in our room, Augusta could no longer kept her mask on.

"How are we going to rescue them?" she demanded.

"We need to gain more of the King's trust," I proposed.

"Ella!" Augusta had an idea. "We now have access to her. I hate to hurt her, but that's our best bet."

∞ฦฦฦฦฦฦฦฦฦฦฦ∞

Four days before the orb extraction.

We were allowed a little more freedom after the dinner with the King. The perimeter of our activities had increased from our room to within the residential floors of the Castle. Apparently, we succeeded in gaining some trust from the Council, but they were still watchful of our actions. Certainly, we had to work harder to convince them.

As we had promised the King to learn what we could from Ella, Augusta and I requested the soldiers to take us to her. Our unknowing ally may just be our ticket to expand our perimeter even more.

To our surprise, Ella was held in the room just directly below us. Two armed guards guarded her door. Our new black armors of the Master Hunters demanded some degree of respect from the guards. They bowed deeply at the sight of us.

"Lady Ella," one of the guards called into the room. "You have wonderful visitors."

The guards stepped aside. We budged into her room arrogantly, but quickly froze in place when we caught a glimpse of her.

Ella looked nothing like that carefree mess she was before.

"Ah, Master Hunters Hadrian and Augusta." She stood there like a beautiful doll, dressed in a fine light blue dress adored with gem stones. Her thick glasses were gone and her hair was styled with ribbons that matched her dress. She looked the part of a princess, but her mismatched rude attitude suggested she disapproved of our new positions.

"What a pleasure!" she mocked.

"Now you dress more like a Councilman's daughter," Augusta quickly pulled herself together to regain control of the situation. "So let's see you act the role, too."

"And you are acting your roles then?" Ella sneered. "I was too young when you two left to do the Tyrant's dirty work, I regret I didn't recognize your ugly greedy mugs... Oh, I can't believe I led you to the Kreeptons!"

"Listen to yourself!" I snapped back. "Which side are you on?"

"The *good* guys'!" she had every intention to put up a fight. "You corrupted idiots!"

"I pity you. Those Tallects had done quite some work on you." Augusta was not here for a verbal exchange of fire. She kept her cool with the agitated Ella. "Lucky for you, for your father's sake, the generous King is willing to forgive you."

"I don't need pity from you lots!" barked Ella.

"This is no game, Miss Ella." The gentle Augusta

knew how to be mean if she wanted to. She approached Ella with commending pressure, causing the proud lady to back up. She leaned close to the alarmed lady and spoke with a malevolent voice. "Give us the names of the members of the Underground Network, then maybe the King would go easy on your punishment."

"Not in a million moon cycles! I'm not afraid of you!" Ella tried to push back but Augusta was not ready to give way.

"Don't worry, your guilt will be spared." Augusta roughly put her hand on Ella's head, forcing her to tilt back. "A memory erasing enchantment would be perfect to knock some sense back to that pretty head."

"You are not messing with my memory!" She gathered enough strength to pushed Augusta away.

"Oh, it's not for you to say, Miss Ella," I said indifferently.

"How could you betray Kresstan?" Ella had tears in her eyes, frustrated with her helplessness. "Do the days you spent with him really mean nothing?"

"Betray?" Augusta let out a cold laugh. "Loyalty to one about to perish is a joke."

"No...You can't..." Ella's voice was cracking.

"What do you expect for a Tallect Prince? Let him give his kinds hope to escape?" I threw down a few pieces of paper and a quill. "You have till after Kresstan's execution to hand us those names. I suggest you start writing."

We left the room with Ella crying in the corner.

I whispered to Augusta when we got back to our room. "I feel so bad to upset her."

"The less she knows, the safer for her."

"You think that's enough?"

"I don't know. But that little scene should be enough

to give us some more freedom to move around the Castle." Augusta pulled out Lady Kassandra's fake Obsidian key. She slipped it into her inventory as the servants were cleaning up the table that night after the dinner in the Grand Hall. "Time to move onto our next action."

The next step of our plan was to contact Kassandra's father, Professor Kortess, the Obelisk expert scientist. We expressed great interest in the Obelisks' mechanism to the Council and hoped to learn more from the scientist himself.

∞ⁿⁿⁿⁿⁿⁿⁿⁿⁿⁿⁿ∞

Three days before the extraction.

We waited anxiously all morning for the Council's decision on our request to visit Professor Kortess.

"Sir, ma'am," a messenger finally came to our room, "you have been approved."

We immediately departed for our visit.

The Professor worked in the Lab Tower of the Castle, opposing to Wicka's Witch Tower. We learned from the Castle guards that he spent much of his time experimenting in the lab. Occasionally he would head to the Northern Gate to apply his results. Four assisting Kreepton scientists shared the rooms with Kortess at the bottom of the Tower.

We thanked the guard who let us into the Lab and ordered him to stay outside to await further instructions. We gave the door to the Lab a knock and pushed the door open gently.

The inside of the Lab Tower was constructed quite different from the Witch Tower. Instead of spirals of stairs, the whole Lab Tower had a twenty-block tall ceiling to allow the space for experiments. All kinds of strange inventions and devices covered the high walls, accessible only with ladders.

"Hunters..." Kortess gave us a look of despise as we entered the Tower. "What do you want from us?"

"Professor Kortess, we came to learn the science behind the Obelisk," I said politely.

Kortess gave us a closer look and realized who we were. "You! How dare you show up here! You two were the ones who tricked Prince Kresstan and...and my own daughter! You think I don't know?" He turned away from us—the reminders of the fate of his daughter. The other four scientists looked on with hostility on their faces. "The Kreeptons' lives in the Settlement is the only reason you'll still be able to walk out of here in one piece. So, PLEASE LEAVE."

"We know how your hands are tied with the TNT situation." Augusta approached Kortess with her hands up to show she meant no harm. She lowered her voice to a whisper and presented the Underground Network talisman and the fake obsidian key. "That's why we would need your help in understanding the extent of the King's power, so we may have a chance to save the Tallects."

"It's my duplicate!" Kortess softened his manner. "How did you get that?"

"From Kassandra." I said softly, "We thought we could sneak into the King's Chamber and set this decoy to buy time."

"The King would have known as soon as he touches this fake key." Kortess examined his handy work. "It was just an idea, but we don't know how to pull it off."

"If you are willing to listen, we may have a way to carry out an escape plan." Augusta chose her words carefully. "But we cannot do it without knowing full details of the mechanism."

Kortess looked at us in amazement and he knew what he had to do. He told the other scientists to make sure we were not watched and signaled us to his work desk.

"How do I know if this is not another trick?" when he was sure we were alone, Kortess questioned us with narrowed eyes.

"You don't know," I said. "But we are all you've got."

Kortess gave it a thought and silently agreed. "The King is not our biggest threat. It's the old Witch named Wilcara you have to watch out for," he said. "Steve is ambitious, but he's harmless without her."

"We saw her at the Council dinner," I said, "She's rather quiet for such a powerful influence."

"Don't underestimate her," Kortess warned. "When the Kreeptons were declared rulers of Tallect, the Witches were not exactly submissive, but due to their small number, they couldn't do anything."

"Hence, their hate towards the Kreeptons." Augusta understood.

"Correct," Kortess continued. "Some time ago, Wilcara discovered the secrets of the Obelisk. She led a group of Witches to Geb. Here, she met the young and charismatic Steve. She promised him a kingdom upon the destruction of Tallect. They cooperated quite nicely, I'm sorry to say. The Witches had their revenge and Steve became King. He showered his people with richness he took from Tallect and they are happy to support his tyranny."

"So the Obelisk is the key to all these..." I thought out loud.

"That is the case." The professor got busy digging into his notes. "I learned of the Obelisk during the Wars and wrote down my discoveries. I hid them in a temple before I got captured."

"The Kreepton Chronicles!" I realized. "And Prince Kresstan found them!"

"So that's how he ended up here!" Kortess was proud of his contribution but regret soon overcame him, "If only I didn't write them, the Prince would have never find out about the Obelisk and he would still be safe in Tallect."

"But he would never be happy alone," Augusta comforted him.

After a moment of silence, I tried to change up the heavy mood. "So if Wilcara knew the Obelisk technique, then what is your role?"

"To study the different materials." Kortess pulled out a page of his research notes. "Each material carries energy differently, thus produces different frequencies that connects different worlds. The latest one built is made of cobblestones."

"Any idea on what could live in that world?" I tired understanding those notes consist of scribbling of "s".

"A species rare in Tallect and Geb known as Arachnids," Kortess presented a drawing of a creature with eight legs and eight eyes.

"Spiders!" We have encounter one of their nest one time when we went too deep into a mine; almost didn't live to tell about them.

"Yes, dangerous cave creatures," Kortess agreed.

"And you need to wait for a thunderstorm to activate that stone Obelisk?" I tried my best to shake the image of the crawling spiders from my mind.

"No," Kortess showed us a design of a machine that

was placed on the side of the Obelisk. "The Obelisk has been greatly improved since your team of Hunters used it. An electricity generator, one of our latest inventions, produces the same amount of power as a lightning strike."

"Impressive," I said, "And with the Witches' enchantment to make these Obelisk indestructible, King Steve can really send in his armies to conquer the worlds as he pleased!"

"Now the enchantment is the key," Kortess said. "Without it, there won't be a retreat for the army if things don't go as planned."

"How have the King been collecting all those orbs for the enchantment?" I asked.

"The Hunters obtained them from the lives of Tallects," Kortess said with great pain. "The first five thousand orbs were used to enchant the Sandstone Obelisk that leads to Tallect..."

Augusta and I waited quietly, wondering if he would be able to continue.

"In hopes that they would spare the lives of the remaining Tallects, we designed the mob spawners to absorb energy from the environment and create those mobs outside of the City." Kortess controlled his emotions and pulled out another design on his desk. "The King pays enthusiasts to hunt them down for their orbs."

"We certainly met one of those..." Augusta said.

"But that isn't enough!" Kortess clutched his fists in anger. "And now they are going to rob our Prince of his orbs...and Kassandra..."

"We'll do all we could to rescue them." Augusta said firmly.

"I truly appreciate your efforts! And I shall provide

you with everything I know." Kortess gathered himself together once again and started to draw out the area Beyond the Northern Gate. "The Obelisk site is like an isolated island. Its ground is completely surrounded by a Four-block tall obsidian wall, accessible only through an obsidian gate. It's only connection to the City is a thirty-block long enclosed cobble stone walkway. Soldiers stood guard at the Gate at all times. The mob generators I mentioned are placed outside all along the obsidian walls. Any attempt to get into the grounds without using the Gate would require intense fighting with the mobs, which would raise alarms from the City guards.

"In other words, enter by invitation only," I said.

"I hate to say it, but the Prince and my daughter's extraction is the invitation we need to get in," Kortess said. "Their procedure will have to take place beyond the Northern Gate. An enchanting table is ready next to the newly constructed Cobblestone Obelisk, and connected to it is a large glass tube that's been collecting the orbs."

"We've over heard some guards talking about a grand exhibition to celebrate the Prince's capture," Augusta remembered.

"With all that, not only would we be able to get into the Northern Gate, if we could create enough distraction, the Kreeptons would have a chance to make a run for it," I said.

"How about the Zombies and Skelees?" Augusta was concerned that they would be harm if the Kreeptons were to escape.

"I can assure you that little harm would come to them. The people of Geb thought of them as nothing more than skilled craftsmen," the professor explained. "Kreeptons, on the other hand, have been portrayed as vicious and too intelligent for the Human comfort."

The next thing we knew, we came up with an escape plan so daring that I didn't know if we would even survive. But at this point, if we didn't take a drastic course of action, there was no doubt that King Steve and the Witches were just slowly going to eliminate the Kreeptons one by one.

"We have to get a message out to Kresstan and the other Kreeptons," I said.

Augusta noticed the fake key and the talisman that were sitting on the desk and had an idea. "I think these just got a whole new purpose."

We left Kortess' lab that evening with a plan in our heads and messages newly inscribed in the squiggly writings of the Kreeptons on the key and the talisman.

Chapter 13:
The Preparations

When we returned to our room from the Lab Tower, a patrolling guard informed us we had a visitor. A shadow with a pointed hat was sitting in a chair in our room as we entered.

"What did we do to deserve your presence, Madam Wilcara?" Augusta greeted the most influential Witch in Geb with a smile.

"What is that you can learn from Kortess that you

cannot learn from me?" Wilcara stood up from the chair, ignoring our politeness, and cut right to the chase.

"A Kreepton's perspective of the whole Obelisk operation," I answered calmly as a matter of fact.

"And he's willing to tell you anything?" Wilcara asked suspiciously.

"With the lives of the remaining Kreeptons at stake, he did," I said victoriously. "Those Kreeptons are too soft, the King's TNT set up is very effective."

"I see. You two knew about the TNTs. You have certainly learned a lot about how things work around here in such a short time," she said coldly. "And surely not wasting time to get yourselves noticed."

"We do have a lot to catch up, madam," Augusta said enthusiastically. "May we ask the reason for your visit?"

"The King called for a meeting." Wilcara glanced at us in annoyance like she couldn't believe the King would pay us any attention. "And he requested your presence."

"We are honored by the King's value of us." Augusta smiled. "And we are thrilled to have you escort us yourself."

"I came to see if I can find any incriminating evidence in your lodgings." Wilcara looked around our simple room with few possessions. "Everything looks clean...so far..."

"I don't know what you were expecting to find," I said innocently with a shrug and changed the subject. "Let's not keep the King waiting."

We curtsied to let Wilcara lead the way. Before we stepped out the door, the old Witch turned and stared back into our eyes from half a block away.

"Just because the King wants to be in friendly terms with you doesn't mean I share the same sentiment.

Don't try any funny business!" with a low warning tone, she added, "I'll be watching."

"Absolutely!" I replied. "We only have the best interest of Geb in mind."

"Though it may not be agreeable with you," I kept that second part to myself.

∞ꊣꊣꊣꊣꊣꊣꊣꊣꊣꊣꊣ∞

We went all the way to the Grand Hall without exchanging another word with the Witch.

In the Grand Hall, we joined the Council and took our place at the long table. The meeting was about making final preparation for the extraction.

Despite Wilcara's protest and wanting to keep things quiet, the other Councilmembers thought it would be an excellent opportunity to display the final triumph over Tallect. The idea of a parade was bought up.

"The pair of Kreepton prisoners should be paraded in chains on their way to the Northern Gate," a Councilman named Elfen suggested. "They should pass by the Settlement with an announcement made to the rest of the Kreeptons as a warning."

"We should make this as festive as the Founding Fest." Captain Famosa made sure his men's efforts were recognized. "Our soldiers fought very hard to bring the Tallects to their knees!"

All these suggestions were perfect! These arrangements would fit in perfectly with our escape plans. With all those people in the streets, the guards would be concentrated in keeping order, setting the stage up for us to rescue the Tallects. If I didn't know the Councilmembers were die hard loyalists to the King, I would think they were on our side, arranging all these for

~91~

our benefits.

"Such motivating designs." King Steve was feeling invincible considered the last time Geb had a festival, he was able to capture the Kreepton Prince. "The improved and more advanced Obelisk has been kept hidden from the public long enough. I think it is time for our people to share all its glory and be inspired to join the conquest of other worlds out there."

The meeting continued with the delegation of the jobs for that day. Wilcara and Wicka would be at the Obelisk making some preparation for the extraction and the subsequent enchantment; Captain Famosa would lead the parade; Councilman Elfen would be responsible for taking Ella to the Northern Gate and sending her back to the Castle afterwards; Other members would ensure everything ran smoothly and uninterrupted by any possible rebellious acts.

Augusta and I volunteered to make an announcement at the Settlement. Our bravery of putting ourselves at the mercy of our captives certainly received some admiration from the Council. No one knew for sure if the Kreeptons would be desperate enough to make a crazy move under the circumstances that their Prince was about to be executed. And we were, as the whole Kingdom now knew, the fearless Hunters who delivered the Tallect royalty to Geb.

While everyone was in a jolly happy mood, I made a request to the King. "Augusta and I wish to pay one last visit to the Kreepton Prince, if Your Majesty will allow."

"And what purpose will that served?" Wilcara said with displease.

"To break whatever resisting spirits they might still have," I stated.

"Ah, you would like to play the doomsday

messenger." King Steve was amused. "Your wish is granted. I look forward to see the defeated look on that proud Kreepton's face. I heard you did some work on Miss Ella, too."

Councilman Quebo startled and almost dropped the quill he was holding at the mention of his daughter. He calmed his nerve and pretended to continue writing while he kept an ear open to our conversation with the King.

"Yes, my King, I'm confident that in time, she'll break and give us those names," I said, trying not to pay too much attention to the worried Councilman. "I trust then, Madam Wicka will make her one of us again."

"That's excellent." The King took a sip of his drink, closed his eyes, and sank into his chair in satisfaction. Wilcara, on his right, rather had the look of a disapproving parent looking at her misbehaving child. There was a good chance that the King would be receiving a lecture from her very soon.

Before we left the dinner party, we got a hold of Captain Famosa. We asked him to allow us to see the Garrison for a little remembering of our old training days.

To our surprise, he agreed right away.

∞ꑷꑷꑷꑷꑷꑷꑷꑷꑷꑷꑷ∞

Two days before the extraction.

We arrived at the Garrison with Captain Famosa early in the morning. The Garrison was where we were initially trained to be soldiers. It certainly brought back some memories. How naïve we were to be used as the King's pawn!

A group of young cadets was practicing their sword

technics on the gravel-covered training ground. The King was readying a new generation of soldiers to fight the next war he planned to wage against the new world he found. Many would repeat our mistakes if we could not complete our mission.

Captain Famosa introduced us to the young cadets and we were welcomed as heroes with great enthusiasm. Apparently, our time in Tallect was made into a legend of some sort and used as a propaganda to inspire the cadets.

"You two survived in the Tallect world for hundreds of moon cycles!" one cadet said.

"I heard you each accumulated hundreds of orbs for the King!" another joined in.

"Please don't give us too much credit, we were just doing what we do best." I don't know how much these young minds had been brainwashed by the King's ideals, but we had to play along for the time being. "With proper training under such great guidance like Captain Famosa's, I'm certain you will do great things for our people soon enough."

The cadets were not ready to end their interviews, but we certainly had a more pressing mission.

We made the excuse to take a tour of the Garrisons, leaving the Captain to his work with the cadets.

As instructed by Professor Kortess, we pretended to wander aimlessly to disguise our intention of heading towards a particular room.

Our task: to disable the TNT buried under the Settlement.

Located on the top of the northwest tower, overlooking the whole Garrison, the Control Room was where the TNT ignition trigger was located. The Room was glowing in dim red stone light. Various signaling devices were all connected to the control panels in that small space.

A young soldier with a serious look was surrounded by more than a dozen switches.

We entered the room and nodded to the young soldier. Our Master Hunter armors quickly demanded him to salute us nervously.

"What is this place here?" I played dumb.

"The Control Room, sir," he answered anxiously. "We receive orders from the Castle here and send instructions to the rest of the Garrison accordingly."

The Castle was clearly in sight just beyond the Settlement through a window in the Room. "What a view!" Augusta engaged him.

"Yes, you can see any signal that comes from the Castle very clearly," the soldier explained to us.

"So, can you see the Settlement from here too?" Augusta pulled the soldier to the window enthusiastically to look outside. "What else can you see?"

I quickly took out a thin coal chip that Kortess gave us and slickly inserted it into one of the switches while the soldier was distracted.

"Oh that is such a breathtaking view, Hadrian," Augusta turned over to me as I was finishing my task.

"Really?" I walked over to the two of them. "But perhaps we shouldn't bother the young soldier for too long."

"Right." Augusta smiled to him.

We thanked the soldier for his time as he saluted us again. To lessen the suspicion for our particular interest in the Control Room, we took our time to greet everyone and pretended to take interest in various devices and proceedings everywhere.

Before we parted with the Captain that afternoon, he

handed us the scroll of announcement we were to read at the Settlement. "Practice well," he said, "and give those Kreeptons a memorable chapter in their history."

The day before the extraction.

We had one last prep work to do, that was a trip to the prison underneath the Castle. We crafted two mini sand Obelisks to serve as Kresstan and Kassandra's mocking "last meals" and arranged to deliver them to the prisoners. Although the King seemed to trust us, Wilcara made sure she had eyes on our every move. A guard, likely a spy for the Witch, carried the treats for us to the Prince's cell.

The prison was dark and damp. Prison cells built out of iron bars lined up on the two sides of a cold bared cobblestone walkway of three blocks wide. A single one-block fenced window at the end of the walkway was the only source of light that came into the prison. A grumpy warden received us and took us to the Tallects' cells.

"Let me explain!" A Human prisoner banged on the iron bar for attention as we made our way down the walkway. "I am absolutely loyal to the King!"

"Get back!" the warden threatened the prisoner with his wooden sword. "Your guilt will be determined by the Council!"

Deeper into the prison, we saw Lady Kassandra curled up in the corner of her cell. She didn't react to our presence. Kresstan was imprisoned in the cell next to hers.

"Greetings, Prince Kresstan," Augusta addressed our Tallect friend as we entered his cell.

"Black armors. You finally found your place

amongst the Tyrant's ranks," Kresstan said, barely looking in our direction. His arms were chained to the back wall of his cell.

"Our memories were affected and we've made some mistakes," Augusta said. "The King is kind and generous. I say it's your Kreepton rulers that should be blamed for your sorry state now."

"Our rulers? Don't you dare twist the facts around! That Tyrant..." Kresstan protested. "I was such a fool to believe in the two of you!"

I interrupted Kresstan rudely with my hand to his face. "Enough insult to the King!" I said. "If Kreeptons were such righteous rulers, why would the Witches take side with the people of Geb to destroy your world?"

"The Witches betrayed us!" Kresstan protested. "They are using you Humans! They can't be trusted!"

"Don't get all worked up, we all have our parts to play," I said lightly. "Perhaps you have learned about your part in the King's plans?"

"Let me guess, a certain death?" Kresstan replied with indifference.

"You'll be contributing your orbs—and your life to enchant a new Obelisk," I said proudly.

"My orbs? Enchant an Obelisk?"

"Such enchantment would make the Obelisk indestructible and it'll serve as the portal for our next expedition to a whole new world." I waved the guard to bring over the sand Obelisks. "We thought your last meals should be symbolic."

Up until now, Lady Kassandra remained immobile. She finally lifted up her head upon hearing about the orbs but could only stared in shock from her curled-up position. Kresstan gave a disgusted look. Anger and humiliation muted him.

"Perhaps the Witches are schemers, but they did give Geb the greatest gift—the secret of the Obelisk," Augusta said as she laid down the plates of sand sculptures on the floor in front of Kresstan. "And they have bought in great improvements. The splendid of Geb will soon spread to many other worlds."

"Other worlds?" Kresstan was astonished to learn of the Obelisk's uses but quickly realized others would suffer the fate of Tallect. "Have you no conscience! How could you do such to others as the Tyrant did to Tallect?"

"Oh don't give us the moral talk! It's just natural for the strong and powerful to conquer the weak," I said. "I suggest you enjoy your last meal, you'll be needing all your strength tomorrow for your big day."

"You can take my life, Human, but do not insult me!" Kresstan wouldn't be able to restrain himself from attacking us if he wasn't restricted by the chain.

"For old time's sake, Kresstan! Don't make this difficult." Augusta pulled the sneering prince up close by his collar and gave him a good eye contact. Then she pushed Kresstan back down to the hard stone floor. "Resistance at this point is meaningless."

"I trusted you!" Kresstan was heartbroken. "*We* trusted you..."

"Well, you shouldn't have," I said.

"Enjoy your presents," Augusta looked gently into the eyes of Lady Kassandra for a good second and glanced down at the Obelisks before turning back to Kresstan, "and enjoy your last day."

"The Kreeptons will not go down without a fight!" Kresstan yelled as we stepped out of his cell for one last attempt to show a fighter's spirit.

I gave him one more look and said quietly, "I'd like

to see you try."

Chapter 14:
The Parade

If our provoking worked, whether Kresstan would smacked his last meal into pieces or actually consume it, he would find our message to him—"Comply but have hope"—an inscription in Kreepton edged by Kortess on the fake obsidian key hidden in the mini Obelisk.

We had planted the seeds of our plan the best we could. The time to set everything in motion was approaching. We had one last seed to plant in the morning. If succeeded, the Kreeptons would have a chance to escape; if failed, all the Kreeptons and probably ourselves would perish under the wrath of King Steve and the Witches.

We took out the announcement scroll Captain Famosa gave us and transformed it into our friendly message to the Kreeptons. We wrapped a few small daggers inside the scroll and covered it up with the Network talisman on the side. It was the perfect prop.

That night passed slowly. We played our rescue plan over and over again in our heads silently in our room, rested little, awaited for the sun to rise in the horizon. We only had one chance to set things right.

A ray of soft daylight eventually shinned through our

window.

"It's time," I said softly.

∞רירירירירירירירירירירי∞

We stepped out of our room looking all splendid and proud.

It was an unusually cloudy morning in Geb, but that didn't affect the festive spirits of the people. Crowds mingled at the market square in front of the Castle in anticipation of the parade. A large orange banner that read "FINAL VICTORY OVER TALLECT" hanged over the façade above the stores at the square. On the rail off to the side, an oversized minecart carrying an iron cage was ready to receive the prisoners.

Under the curious eyes of the spectators, Kresstan and Kassandra were brought out to the square by Captain Famosa and a dozen guards. The prisoners seemed calm and cooperative, and not a sign of despair. While the Kreeptons were getting chained to the inside of the cage like subdued animals, people pointed and gossiped noisily. They were excited to catch a glimpse of that Prince who took a few hundred moon cycles to capture.

Councilman Elfen also made his way to the square with Ella. Although she was not bound in anyways, the Councilman never let go of her arm.

"Turncoats!" Ella muttered under her breath when she saw us.

We pretended not to hear her and proceeded to greet the Councilman.

Then when all was set, the King made his entrance into the market square. He climbed up a stage in front of the Castle. We stood by the stage and waited. My inside felt like a fired up sparkling red stone circuit, but I did my best to cover it.

"Nervous?" Captain Famosa came over to us after he settled the prisoners. His large rough hand put some pressure on my shoulder like he did in our Hunter days. "Don't worry. Everything will go as planned."

I wish I could wholeheartedly accept the Captain's reassurance. He was once a father figure to Augusta and me. It was so easy to just listen and follow everything he said. But that was in the past. This time, we were on our own trying to save another civilization.

This time, he was our enemy.

The King cleared his voice with a cough and the crowd went silent.

"My loyal subjects," King Steve began, "I'm thrilled to officially announce that we have the Kreepton Prince in our possession. Their tyranny and oppression towards our ally, the Witches, can finally be a thing in the past!"

The people cheered excitingly. But we didn't share their enthusiasms.

"Tyranny and oppression!?" I whispered to Augusta.

"I'm sure you know a whole different story." Captain Famosa was eavesdropping next to us. "But that's been the story the King tells the people to gain their support in his aggressions against Tallect."

We looked at the Captain with a questionable look. His opinion towards the King seemed to have changed with his use of the word "aggressions." Was there something else he had not been telling us?

"I cannot thank my two brave Hunters enough for their assistance in this achievement," the King continued his speech as the cheers subsided. He gestured us to come on stage. "Please show your gratitude for Master Hadrian and Master Augusta!"

Another round of cheers and applause. We shyly got up to the stage to give a bow and wave to thank the people and hurried in getting back down. We just wanted this to be over quickly.

"Shortly, I will also reveal the greatest gift the Witches have given to Geb," the King said with pride. "It will allow us to continue to thrive and bring more riches to our people!"

The crowd were chatting excitingly, guessing what this gift was.

The King went on to give a few more credits to his Council and showed his appreciation to the people. Kresstan simply stood in his cage void of any expression with Kassandra leaning on him for support. Our sights crossed for a brief moment. There was no sign of anger in his eyes like when we last saw him in the prison cell. Knowing Kresstan, he would not have been able to remain this calm. Unless, he had seen the message.

"Without further delay, let the parade begin!" King Steve announced and the crowd cheered and gave way to a ban of drummers and flute musicians, followed by the King, a train of soldiers, and the cage of prisoners. We tailed at the very end of the line with Captain Famosa.

The parade passed through a few major streets in the City. Wave after wave of people came to check out the captive like he was a rare and magical creature. The King had portrayed Kresstan as this mystical monster, so his triumph would seem more amazing.

While the Kreeptons were splashed with dirt and rotten food launched from the people, Augusta and I, on the other hand, received salutes and cheers. We forced out smiles and waved to reply this fanfare.

At last, our train halted in front of the Garrison. Augusta, Captain Famosa, a handful of guards, and myself went inside. The cage was left outside the Garrison, guarded by armed soldiers. People gathered behind a fence outside the Garrison, trying to take a peek at the ceremony. Regular citizens were not allowed to follow into the Garrison for safety reasons. The Kreepton Settlement was, after all, filled with TNTs.

With the go signal from the Captain, Augusta and I pushed the button to the double iron doors of the Settlement. With the announcement scroll in my hand, we invited ourselves into the angry pack of Kreeptons.

"Kreeptons of Tallect," as soon as I walked in, I opened up the scroll, addressed the group of furious faces that were about to turn from green to red. Augusta kept her hand on the sword at her waist and readied to draw it at the first sign of danger. "I came to deliver an announcement from the King."

"We should have followed our instinct and not let you two out the last time you set foot in here!" one Kreepton yelled.

"I understand your anger, but any foolish actions would not save your Prince now," Augusta said as she put up a hand to stop the soldiers outside the doors from advancing in for our protection.

"I rather die!" another said.

The Kreeptons were getting agitated.

"And let the last of you be killed?" Augusta challenged. "Go ahead! Take on Geb in your sorry state!"

The Kreeptons backed down, painfully agreed with Augusta that they were not in a position to fight back.

I took the moment of silence to begin reading from the scroll.

"By the order of King Steve of the Kingdom of Geb, Kresstan, Prince of Kreeptons of Tallect, was found guilty of his cruelty to his subjects in his home world of Tallect and upon his subjects' escape to Geb, he followed them in an attempt to do further harm. His selfish actions had knowingly caused unrest in the Kingdom of Geb. It was great fortune that he was stopped and arrested before additional damages could be done. To answer for his crimes, he is sentenced to death Beyond the Northern Gate. His life force will be contributed to the greater good of Geb. His accomplice, a Kreepton by the name of Kassandra, shall suffer the same fate. Let their punishments be an example set for any Tallect who wishes to repeat their wrong doings in the future. These are the messages from His Majesty, King Steve."

"Cruelty? Harm?" Outrage was stirring up again in the green crowd. "Those are the words of those treacherous Witches!"

A Kreepton fist almost reached my face, but Augusta blocked it just in time. She pushed the aggressor back into the crowd.

"Save your strength for something else." I stepped forward and handed a calm old Kreepton the scroll with the Network talisman facing him.

From that trace of surprised expression, it was safe to assume that the old Kreepton recognized the talisman. He reached out to take the scroll. As soon as he felt the unusually heavy weight of the supposed stick-and-paper, he was certain we were no enemies.

"Elder Kossac!" a Kreepton yelled. "How could you accept these ridiculous accusations towards the Prince and the Lady?"

"We still have work to do here in Geb," despite his age, Elder Kossac spoke with a powerful voice. "Let these soldiers do what they are meant to do."

As unwilling as they were, they obeyed their Elder and let us out of the Settlement peacefully.

Chapter 15:
Beyond the Northern Gate

When we exited the Garrison, the people who waited anxiously outside were quite glad to see us. Whether they were happy because we survived the mob of Kreeptons or that they got to continue the spectacle, I didn't bother to find out. We rejoined the parade at the very end, worried about those Kreeptons. Did we really send them a pass to freedom or a curse worse than death?

The train continued to proceed down the rail. At last, we arrived at the Northern Gate.

A pair of rather plain iron doors marked the entrance to the all-secretive section of the Kingdom.

The small six-block-wide clearing in front of the Gate was nothing more than some excess space in the back of a few buildings. On regular days, the area hardly got any foot traffic. But today, every block there was jammed up. More victory banners of various colors decorated the city wall and the buildings next to the iron doors.

"Everything is on schedule, Your Majesty," Captain Famosa reported.

"Excellent." The King smiled satisfyingly. "Let us

proceed to our next event."

Somehow, a small platform managed to squeeze into that tiny clearing for the King. Always a show, he certainly never missed a chance to perform.

"Behold, citizens of Geb," the King announced, "the gift from our allies!"

The King raised his hand. Following the direction he pointed, we saw a few Witches on top of the city wall busy working on something.

The spectators looked up too, wondering about this "gift."

As the King dropped his hand down, the fog that enclosed Beyond the Northern Gate evaporated. The upper portion of a Sandstone Obelisk enveloped in colorful enchantment glow stood magnificently beyond the city wall. Just a little further, stood another one of that skyscrapers in dull grey.

The spectators went wild! Chatting and gasping filled the air. And like streams of wind, people's amazement blown through the city. Given the height of the Obelisks, they could be seen hundreds of blocks away.

"The Obelisk will be free to use by all citizens as soon as we perfected a few final techniques," the King said to the electrified crowd.

"Now, we shall finish what we came to do." The King nodded to the Captain and stepped down from his small platform. "Let us proceed to the Gate, gentlemen."

The Captain went to the cage to unchain the Kreeptons and led them on.

King Steve shot a look at the prisoners with a smirk. "Ready to meet your end?" he said to Kresstan.

Kresstan was not about to give the King the pleasure to insult him in front of the people and chose to keep his silence.

"What's wrong? You ran out of words?" The King was not thrilled with Kresstan's snubbing.

"You'll have the pleasure of watching these Kreeptons suffer soon enough, Your Majesty," Captain Famosa jumped in to rescue the awkward moment. He invited the King to head for the doors.

Without further delay, the King led the way through the pair of iron doors, followed by the prisoners, the Captain, Councilman Elfen and Ella, and two other soldiers. Augusta and I trailed at the very end again. One by one, we stepped into the dim stone tunnel. The doors behind us closed gently.

The walls surrounding the city was a good five blocks thick. It protected the citizens from the mobs outside, but the wall of this tunnel we were in was merely one stone layer thick. In the tunnel, calls of the mindless zombies and sound of rattling bones of the skeletons were leaking through the thin wall, echoing down the tunnel, sending chills down the spines of the travelers. The dense forest outside the City must had shielded the mobs from catching the sun, allowing them to survive in bright daylight. With danger larking at such close proximity, the thirty-block walk felt like a three-hundred-block journey.

"Very soon, a much larger tunnel will replace this, so our grand army will be able to match to the next world!" King Steve spoke his mind loudly, trying to lessen the creepiness.

"That will be splendid!" Councilman Elfen resonated the King's enthusiasm.

The tunnel finally came to an end. As expected, a barred gate made of deep purple obsidian stood between us and the Obelisks. Black glass panels filled all the gaps the obsidian material did not cover. It was rather difficult to see through. The Northern Gate was transparent and solid at the same time.

The King reached into his pocket and took out the real obsidian key. It was wrapped in an enchanted glow. He inserted the key into the keyhole of the Gate and gave it a small turn.

Ka-cha...a...a... The sound of the slowly opening Gate resonated down the tunnel.

Light flooded into our eyes, blinding us momentarily. The slowness of the Gate opening and the transition from darkness to light must be part of the design to secure the area against intruders. Whoever tried to enter the Gate uninvited would surely be hindered by these features, allowing guards to capture them.

As our visions adjusted, the swaying multi-colored Sandstone Obelisk dominated our view. It was placed right in the middle of about four hundred square blocks of space contained by obsidian walls and even a floor.

"Impressive, isn't it?" the Captain commented to Augusta and me. "The whole chamber becomes the portal when the Obelisk is activated, taking everyone and everything to the other world within the obsidian premises.

"Have you used it?" I asked.

"I did a test run with a few other Hunters when it was finished." The Captain recalled. "It was a much smoother ride than the un-enchanted version."

The King marched past the Sandstone Obelisk and headed to another obsidian gate in the back of the Sandstone Obelisk chamber. He used the same key to open the second gate.

As the gate slowly swung open, a disgusting all-too-familiar smell leaked through the gate.

"Yuck! What is that smell!" Ella couldn't help but to exclaim. "I want to spill my guts out!"

"That is exactly what it does," I told Ella as she looked at me with bewildered eyes.

Trying our best to ignore the smell, we stepped into the second chamber. It had the exact same layout as the first, except the Obelisk in this one was made of cobblestones. This chamber also featured a ten-block tall glass tube, half-filled with orbs glowing in mesmerizing lights. An enchantment table in front of the Obelisk was connected to the tube.

Surrounding the enchantment table were Wilcara, Wicka, and another young Witch. They were finishing their set up. A cauldron full of those unmistakable lime green goo was set close to them.

"All is ready to perform the extraction," Wilcara addressed the King in routine business-like manners.

"Gr...Great..." the King had been covering his mouth and nose, trying very hard to hold his breath to minimize breathing in the stench. "Ack! I've never imagined how repulsive those potions smell. I'm getting out of here as soon as the procedure is under way!"

"Very well, Your Majesty," Wilcara said. "This will take half a day anyway, Wicka and I will head back with you to the Castle. The rest shall stay to finish the job."

"Let's get this going quickly then," the King signaled Captain Famosa to proceed.

The Captain and the other soldiers took Kresstan and Kassandra by the chains and bound them up back to back onto the glass tube with their hands still tied behind.

"Professor!" Wilcara called to the Obelisk. "Any last words with your daughter?"

Professor Kortess emerged from behind the Obelisk

and moved towards his daughter.

"Father!" Kassandra was surprised but thrilled to see him.

He cupped her square face and gave her a good look. "All will be well soon. I will take care of things."

"I know...We know," the Lady said softly.

"Enough delay! It won't change anything!" the King complained. "I need to breathe again!"

The Kreeptons gave the King a nasty look. Captain Famosa pulled Kortess away from his daughter and set him next to us.

Wicka filled a bottle with the green goo. She went up to Kresstan with the young Witch following.

"You two make such a beautiful couple...Couple thousands of orbs! Hehehe..." Wicka laughed at her own pun with her screeching high pitch voice. "Gentleman first, shall we?"

"Witches! You'll answer for your wrong to the Tallects soon enough!" As a resistance, Kresstan stepped on Wicka's foot so hard that she almost dropped the bottle in pain.

Wicka was so mad that her face turned red. Without another word, she reached into her robe and threw a potion at Kresstan. And the Prince's body instantly became stiff.

"We'll have your legs tied too in a moment!" She shook up her aching foot to regain some feelings to it. Her assistant then forced open the Prince's mouth as Wicka roughly shoved the bottle of goo into his mouth.

Even though less than a quarter of the goo went down Kresstan's throat, his body, though stiff, reacted already. Before Kresstan could take a breath, a stream of colorful glowing orbs shot out of his mouth into the air, he let out a cry in pain as the glass tube behind him glowed brighter and sucked in all his orbs.

I remembered that feeling of the orbs gushing out all too well and couldn't help but felt his agony.

Kassandra held Kresstan's hands tightly from behind in hopes to lessen her friend's pain. Ella couldn't bear to watch. She turned her head to the side and sobbed quietly. The Witches and the King, however, were entertained by this torture.

After the longest clicks in my life, the upward flow of light stopped, Kresstan was finally able to take some shallow breaths. One of the guards went up to bind his legs to prevent any more assault to the executioner.

"Looks like this is going to take even longer than expected." Wicka examined her victim's extracted orbs in the glass tube. "There's just so many orbs!"

"As amusing as this is, let's head back for now." The King's nose detected the smell again once the excitement paused. "We need to prepare the books and the lapis for the enchantment."

Wicka handed the remaining potion to the young Witch and made her way to join Wilcara and the King.

"Start on the Lady when you finished that bottle. She won't take as long to empty out," Wicka ordered the young Witch.

"We shall expect you for dinner, gentlemen," the King said as he was hasting out the obsidian gate.

The moment the gate shut, Kresstan's extraction resumed. The young Witch did not dare to slow down and mess up her assignment.

We endured two more rounds of the extraction painfully so that we could be sure the King and the Witches were out of the Northern Gate. By the third round, the bottle of potion was almost gone. We couldn't be sure if Kresstan could survive another one.

I looked to Augusta and muttered, "you get the Witch, I'll hold off the Captain and the soldiers, then..."

Before I could say another word, Captain Famosa went up to the unsuspecting Witch and eliminated her in one stroke of his sword. Her orbs were quickly sucked into the glass tube.

What just happened?

"WHAT ARE YOU TWO WAITING FOR?" the Captain yelled.

He just gave us an order!

We quickly pulled out our swords and took out the shocked soldiers before they could sort out the confusion. Their orbs, too, contributed to the glass tube.

Just as I was approaching Councilman Elfen to take him out, the Captain blocked me in my path with his sword. "He's one of us," he said.

"Who's us?" Augusta pointed her sword at the Councilman.

"The Network." The Captain took out from his pocket the talisman of the same design as the one from Zella. The Councilman presented the same.

Ella grabbed the talismans from the men and inspected them carefully.

"It's the true talisman of the Network," Ella declared.

"Captain, you..." I wanted to inquire but the Captain stopped me.

"Time for questions later, we need to act fast before the Witches notice the stream of orbs stopped," the Captain commended. "The obsidian gates lock on one side automatically when they close. You can exit without the key, but won't be able to get back in. So, Hadrian, Augusta, hold the gates for me while I go to the tunnel to slow down any pursuit. Professor, set up the Obelisk for use. Councilman and Ella, free the Kreeptons and take all the weapons and potions dropped by our victims."

"Yes, sir!" we responded.

Captain Famosa just took over as the commander of our operation. With his expertise, we were glad he did!

The Captain zoomed out of the Cobblestone Obelisk chamber as Augusta held the gate open. Then he and I ran past the Sandstone Obelisk to the Northern Gate. He pulled out a TNT and Flint and steel as he got close to the Gate.

"Hold the door just big enough for me and close it as soon as I'm back in," the Captain ordered me.

Without another word, he plunged into the dark tunnel and placed the block of TNT halfway in there. In a swift motion, he set it off. As the explosive block sizzled, he turned and ran as fast as he could to dive back through the gate. With all my power, I forced the normally slow-closing gate to a shut just in time to shield the explosion.

"Without the tunnel, the mobs would bury the path and slow down anyone approaching the gate." The Captain dusted his armor.

We hurried back through the second gate Augusta was holding and back into the Cobblestone Obelisk chamber.

When we got in, Kresstan and Kassandra were released from their bondage. But Kresstan was too weak to stand by himself and was barely conscious. Kassandra and Ella were supporting him while the Councilman picked up the last of the items floating on the ground.

"The Obelisk is ready," Professor Kortess reported from his post next to a switch, which I assumed was the electrical device for activating the Obelisk.

"Good," the Captain said. "Everyone, fasten your weapons well but keep them at an easy reach, we don't know where we'll land."

"Wait! Where are we going?" Kassandra asked.

"To the Arachnid world," Professor Kortess further explained our plan. "It may be riskier than using the Sandstone Obelisk, but this un-enchanted portal would explode upon use. It'll buy us some time before the King can rebuild it and come after us."

"No more talk! Our tricks won't hold the King's army for long." The Captain hurried us. "Professor, on my mark..."

At the signal of the Captain, the Professor pulled the switch.

An electrical charge shot down from the tip of the Obelisk to its base. At the sound of the four explosions at the bottom of the massive structure, everything was consumed.

The white light of the blasting TNTs was blinding. I heard the glass of the tube shattering. The last thing I saw before my sight completely went out was the orbs scattered in mid-air and rushed towards every one of us. An intense feeling of warmth grew in me and everything went blank...

Chapter 16:
The Arachnid World

My senses returned bit by bit.

The first thing I felt was cold...and wet...?

"Embrace yourselves for the fall!" the muffled voice sounded like Kresstan.

Before I could call out to him, water rushed into my mouth and nose. I managed to take a breath above the moving water. It was so dark I couldn't even see my own hands.

"Ahhh!"

One by one, I heard screams coming from in front of me and disappearing into some distance below.

We landed right next to a waterfall! And it was my turn to plunge into the pit below!

"Ahhh!"

SPLASH!

I fought my way to the surface of the river at the bottom of the fall. It was still pitch black. The fast - flowing water rammed me into a block and I held on to it. Someone else also found my block.

"Ella?" I felt her long smooth hair flowing my way.

"Hadrian!" She was relieved to have found me in this darkness.

I then noticed a dim yellow light just a few blocks down stream. Captain Famosa was just visible in the soft light. He placed down a block of glow stone. Soon, we were assembled at its guidance.

"Do we have everyone?" The Captain did a head count. "Is everyone alright?"

"Looks like we all still have our limbs," Ella said.

"How are you feeling, Kresstan?" Augusta checked on our friend who had just been through torture.

"Quite well, rather." Kresstan stretched his body and flexed his arms. "I believe a number of the orbs were returned to me when the glass tube broke."

"I think we all got some of those, too," Kortess said.

"That explains why I feel more...alive." I was not sure how to describe that feeling of a new level of energy.

Councilman Elfen pulled out a few torches and lighted up our surrounding as we assessed our position. We were standing at a small landing next to a river. Cobblestones were all around us whichever direction we looked.

"It appears we are next to an underground river," the Professor said. "Spiders are cave creatures, we may very well be in their territory."

"In that case, we have to build a base to protect ourselves from possible attacks." Captain Famosa always knew his survival protocols. "And then we'll evaluate and figure out our next action."

We pulled out a few pickaxes from our inventories and started digging into the wall where we were.

"So, Captain, since when did you become a member of the Network?" While we worked on the base, Augusta finally brought up the question we had been wanting to ask.

"Long before your return," the Captain answered without stopping his construction. "You really think those little tricks you played would save the Tallects?"

"I knew it! Everything was just too easy!" I said. "You are on our side all along!"

The Captain chuckled at our realization.

"How come I didn't know about all these?" Ella recognized that she was the only one who didn't have the slightest idea of anything. "In fact, you Hunters were beyond mean to me!"

"It's for your protection," Councilman Elfen said as he placed down some freshly crafted fences. "The less people knew, the safer kept the secret."

"And with those careless actions of yours, how could

we trust you with something this important?" The Captain had little regards for the lady's feelings.

"I'm not *that* careless..." Ella protested. Augusta and I couldn't help but laugh in agreement with the Captain.

"Nevertheless, you *are* a great inventor," the Captain added as he placed down a number of Ella's gadgets from his inventory inside our half-completed base. "Like this 'life detector' will certainly locate the spiders fast."

"You have my stuff!" Ella was delighted at the sight of her inventions and jumped in to examine them. "That's why you raided my shop."

"Captain Famosa," Kresstan approached the Captain with a stern face, remembering his defeats in the hands of the Master Hunters. "The last time we saw each other, it was at a fight to the death in Tallect..."

"My deepest apologies. I was, indeed, fooled." The Captain stopped his construction and lowered his head. It was a rare moment that he swallowed his pride and admitted his mistake. "As a soldier, I completely bought into the King's story about the Witches being victims. There's no excuse for my ignorance, but you can be certain that my days of fighting on the wrong side is over."

"Apology accepted. Whatever the reasons, for all that you have done, we are eternally in your debt." Kresstan's stern face melted into a smile. He extended his hands as a gesture to forgive the Captain's actions in the past. "It's an honor to fight along your side this time around, Captain."

"The past will always be the past, but I'm glad to have a chance to make it up to the Tallects." The Captain gave Kresstan's hand a good shake.

"And Hadrian and Augusta," Kresstan turned to us, "please accept my apologies for doubting your friendships!"

"Oh, Kresstan." Augusta gave Kresstan a hug. "We understand."

"And *sorry* for being a bully in the prison!" I added with a smile. "Glad we don't have to pretend anymore!"

"I'm just curious, Captain," Kassandra was still rather skeptical of the Captain and the Councilman's motivations. "May I ask why you have a change of heart? Why would men of your positions take such a risk?"

"Don't think too noble of me. The Councilman and I did it more so for our own people," the Captain said. "After being in the Council, I learned that the Witches were simply using us to take the worlds for themselves."

"I know other Council members are perfectly happy with what richness we have, but I'm just not one of them," the Councilman added. "I would not allow the Witches to risk our people's lives for their gain."

"We have a common enemy then. Our collaboration would bring us to our goal," Kresstan replied.

"It's for the good of both our worlds," the Councilman said.

"The day we rebuild our civilization, your heroic acts will live on in our history," Kortess said.

"If there would still be enough of us left to go on..." Kresstan frowned. "Those Witches will for sure take their rage out on the other Tallects!"

"Don't worry, Kresstan." I nodded to the Professor. "We took care of the TNTs switch with that coal chip the Professor gave us. An elder at the Settlement seemed to realize we were there to help. I'm certain that he had found your message and a few daggers wrapped in the announcement."

"'The message 'TNT disabled. Escape with teleport' was carved on Zella's talisman," Kortess said. "But it's

~118~

still an uphill battle to get out of the city."

"I have arranged a few Network members to assist on that," the Captain said as he laid down the last few blocks of cobblestone for our simple base. "The Kreeptons would be taken to safety, along with the Zombies and Skelees. The other thirty or so Tallects hiding away from the Kingdom will take them in."

"Other Tallects?" The Kreeptons in our party were shocked to learn of other survivors. So were we.

"Yes, they were sent to Geb when your ancient Obelisk was set off," the Captain clarified. "I accidentally came into contact with them and learned the full extent of the Witches' treachery against Tallect."

"What has become of them?" The Professor was eager to learn about the fate of their missing citizens.

"They..." Captain Famosa was interrupted by a sound from outside our just-finished base.

"Spiders!" Professor Kortess recognized their hissings.

"Hunters, ready your weapons." The Captain peaked through the freshly installed door of our base. "Looks like scouts and they've spotted our glow stone. About twenty in number, fifteen blocks out. Hadrian, take the right, Augusta, left, the center is mine."

"Yes, sir!" we answered.

Captain Famosa rushed out the door with his sword ready for battle. Augusta and I splinted to the two sides of him. The spiders reacted at the sight of us. Their sets of eight legs charged them toward us. The Captain used his momentum to jump up and take his first kill. The dead spider's orbs temporary brought light into the landing until they were absorbed by the victor. Augusta and I were not far behind, a few strikes and kicks, we produced our own splashes of orbs.

Three down. Four. Five. Six. And more followed.

The swamp of spiders reduced in number quickly. But they were no easy foes. They backed up and regrouped. Their hissing grew more intense and louder like a battle cry.

Without another warning, they launched a new mode of attack at us. As they charged toward us, they split up and surrounded us in all sides, forcing us to back into each other. We each took on two or three spiders at a time. One threw an attacked with its sharp spear-like limb, then backed off while another took its place before we could make our counter move. We were locked in a defensive position, unable to attack. The spiders were tiring us out with their number.

Two spiders came at me at the same time, I managed to block them with my sword, but my weapon was trapped by them. Their hissing rang in my ears loudly as their fangs inched towards my face. I saw, from the corner of my eye, another one climbed up to the top of the cave and was dropping down on me. Seeing that I had no way out, I ready myself for the blow.

SWOOSH!

An arrow was shot from the direction of our base and took out my air-born attacker.

"Kresstan!" I almost forgot he was a fierce fighter as well.

He took out a few spiders with his arrows, freeing us from our trapped positions.

"My apologies. It took a while to gather all the arrows." Kresstan broke up the circle of spiders surrounding us. Block by block, we pushed the remaining spiders into the river. Some lost their footing and got flushed down the raging water. A few of them managed to hop onto their drowning comrades in the water and got to the other side.

We stood at the edge of the landing, watching the spiders fled. A set of eight red eyes flashed in the cave across the river.

Kresstan shot an arrow at those narrowing eyes, but a long pale object swung at the arrow and broke it in half. Before Kresstan could fire again, the eyes disappeared with the retreating spiders into the darkness.

"They know we are here," Captain Famosa said. "We need to get out of here before they come back with reinforcements."

Chapter 17:
The Maze of Webs

We returned to our short-lived base and informed our party of our emergency situation.

"And I was just getting comfy in this hole!" Ella threw her hands up and rolled her eyes.

The Captain was never the one to enjoy humor. He ignored Ella and proceeded to order us. "Everyone, empty your inventory and we'll redistribute our supplies as needed."

We obeyed the Captain and scattered everything we have on the ground. Looked like we were all quite prepared. Bread, pork chop, chicken, sand, weapons, a number of Ella's odd inventions, TNTs, redstone dust, torches, some wood planks, pickaxes, shovels, and some iron ingots. We divided the food amongst the humans and the sand for the Kreeptons, the weapons to the fighters, the materials to the Professor and Councilman, and Ella had her gadgets back.

We securely stored the items in our inventories and went out the door. It was pitch black and void of life as far as we could see.

"Where should we go?" I asked as I stared into the darkness.

"Follow those spiders," the Captain ordered.

"That's a bit risky, Captain," the Councilman said.

"Have you never heard of keeping your enemies close?" the Captain boldly stated. "Instead of waiting for those spiders to come to us when we are least prepared, we'll take them down in our own terms."

"In fact, that may be what we have to do," the Professor advised. "We have no idea how deep underground we are, and spiders, although are underground creatures, still need to go above ground to get food. So we may be able to find a route to the ground by following them."

While we remained undecided, Kresstan took his stand with the suggestions. "That sounds reasonable, Professor. And I trust your expertise in warfare strategies, Captain."

"Thanks, Prince." The Captain was glad someone agreed with him.

"I go where the Prince goes," Kassandra said.

"It's crazy!" Ella joined in, holding one of her devices. "But I'm always ready to sign up for an adventure! And I know just the gadget for that!"

Ella was holding what looked like a single drawer box with a glass screen on top. We looked on in amazement. She pushed a few buttons to activate the device. "This is a life detection machine," she introduced. As it booted up, spots of light ran wild in all directions on the screen. "Now I just need a piece of the creature we want to detect."

"Here's one." Kassandra picked up a small slimy red-ish purple ball with gooey strings dangling from it.

"Eww... Gross!" Ella pulled open the drawer compartment of the machine to let Kassandra drop that blob of spider eye in. Ella closed the compartment and the machine began to analyze. "Currently it has the range of about a two-hundred-block radius, but I'm working to expand that if I get back to Geb alive."

The lights on the screen started to form a mass of red dots on the top edge.

"Well, the good news is they are less than two hundred blocks away." Ella zoomed in to those red dots. "The bad news is, there are some fifty of them..."

"Let's not waste time then!" While we were so focused on the detection machine, Captain Famosa and Kresstan already started building a simple bridge across the raging river.

"The four of us warriors can take care of a dozen each." Kresstan said as he laid down the last piece of cobblestone for the bridge.

"The two of you work so well together!" The Councilman laughed at the new-found partnership of the former sworn enemies.

We crossed the bridge and headed into the dark tunnel where the group of spiders disappeared into. The Captain led our party, lighting the way with a torch, followed by Kresstan, Augusta and I. Ella was right behind us, checking for spider activities. Lady Kassandra and the Professor were well protected with the

Councilman moving along backwards to secure our rear ends. Those of us with weapons were ready to fight at a split click's notice.

The beginning of the tunnel was a comfortable three-by-two opening, but it narrowed to a two-by-two shaft in just twenty blocks and accompanying turns and raisers. Not only that, spider webs lined the corners of the tunnel. We had to make some body-twisting turns and bands in order to avoid getting stuck to them. The red dots on the detector screen rotated in different sides of the screen at every turn. Then, the path split. The tunnel branched out into three.

"Which way should we go?" the Captain checked with Ella.

"I can't be sure. There were so many turns earlier. The direction here can't be trusted," Ella checked her device and offered no solution.

"The webs," the Professor said from behind the line. "Spiders like to leave webs behind. One is to slow down enemies, and two is to mark territories. The most frequently used path would have the most webs."

"Good call," the Captain said and gave his orders. "Hadrian, Augusta, Kresstan, you each take a torch and go down fifteen to twenty blocks in each tunnel and see if they match the amount of webs we've been seeing."

"Yes, sir!" We each pulled out a torch and headed right in. I took the one on the right, and in just ten blocks, there was a web. I swing my torch forward to look deeper into the path, a turn to the left, and the right. I peeked into the two sides, more webs lined the right. I went further in, more division. This place is like a maze!

I made my way back out and reported my findings.

"Kresstan and Augusta hardly saw any webs in the

other two, so the right one should lead us to the spiders," the Captain said. "And looks like we'll have to continue relying on the webs to guide us."

We took the right tunnel further in. A right, then a left, then a left, and a right again... Some parts of the tunnel only had an opening of two blocks wide and one block high—just enough for a spider to cross. We had to crawl under to get through. Even though the cave creatures were only two hundred blocks away, the distance we had to travel was more like triple that with all those twists and turns. And since we didn't want to attract the attention of fifty spiders, we couldn't just use the pickaxes to dig our way through.

"Stop!" Ella suddenly called. "A group of about twenty is zig zagging very quickly towards our way. It's hard to say how far they are with all those turns they are making."

"Must be reinforcements from earlier," Kresstan suggested.

"Weapons ready!" the Captain ordered. "Back up into one of those web-free tunnels."

We went back the way we came, hid ourselves in the tunnels out of the spiders' path and held our breath. The torch was put away. Even Ella's detecting device was covered up to extinguish every bit of light.

We were left blind in complete darkness. Our hearing kept us informed of the approaching spiders. Their hissing and clicking sound got louder and louder and eventually passed in front of us.

When the last of the spider sound faded away, Ella uncovered her device to check for activities. The group of twenty red dots had moved passed us towards the direction of the landing.

The Captain pointed to the fighters to follow him

and the rest to stay put. He lighted up his torch again and checked around the web filled tunnel. "Looks clear," the Captain whispered to us.

Before we could even take a breath of relieve, the hissing started again and it was coming in from our front and back, even from above us!

We were surrounded and trapped!

Chapter 18:
The Nest

"Stay where you are!" the Captain called out loudly to those of us hiding, masking it as a command to the fighters.

Before long, these smaller, blue-greenish spiders surrounded us. A few came out of trap doors not too far ahead of us.

"Cave spiders!" Augusta recognized the army of the even more vicious creatures. The detector must have failed to pick up cave spiders with the different kind of spider eye. We held up our swords and readied ourselves for an attack.

To our surprise, the army of spiders simply stood there and watched us with their narrow red eyes. Amongst them, a single cave spider stepped forward. It was holding a pure white blade with one of its legs. The texture suggested it was a blade of quartz. It looked like the piece of weapon that broke Kresstan's arrow at the landing earlier.

I didn't know spiders were capable of using any kind of tool. Then again, I didn't know about inventing Kreeptons and talking Zombies before all these either.

"Creatures. From. Geb," although it sounded a bit forced, the spider with the white blade addressed us in our human tongue. He was likely their commander. "Please. Stand. Down. We. Have. Been. Expecting. You."

"You can talk?" And how did they know we were from Geb? I wondered what other surprises these eight-legged monsters of the dark still had.

"A. Little." it replied with difficulty. "Follow. Me. The Witches. Welcome. You."

Captain Famosa seemed to have realized something, he lowered his weapon and whispered to us. "Follow my lead, let me do the talking. I think I know what the deal is."

We did what we were told and put away our weapons. The spiders steered the four of us further down the tunnel like sheep. Many a good number of turns later, we arrived at an opening that looked down some twenty blocks into a large cave full of spiders. The fifty or so red dots on the life detector were an underestimation, there were more like a few hundreds of them engaging in various activities—building rooms within the cave, shoving sheep and cows into a pen, readying them for butchering, a group to the side was practicing using those white blades.

Our tunnel was not the only one that led into the cave, there were dozens of other tunnel openings lining the walls of this cave. This underground world was so full of holes like a giant piece of Swiss cheese.

One by one, the spiders lowered themselves to the floor of the cave using their sticky silk. Their commander hissed out an order in spider tongue to a few of them. Those spiders responded by launching at us! They wrapped us in their legs, then jumped off the edge of the tunnel.

Down we went!

Sheeee...

Sheeee...

Sheeee...

Sheeee...

One by one, we survived the "fall" to the bottom of the cave.

"Wow! That was one insane ride!" Augusta said as her spider vessel released her.

Our presence certainly alarmed the entire cave. Its inhabitants all dropped what they were doing and focused their eight eyes on us. Fortunately, before they made any move on us, their commander landed between us and the agitated mobs. He let out a low frequency warning that forced every one of them to back off. Then he yanked his head to have us follow him across the floor of the cave.

The mass of spiders split to form a path for us. That sea of red spots never released us from their gaze. We did not dare to lag too far behind the commander and just kept our focuses on putting one foot in front of the other.

This game of sudden death finally ended in front of a roughly crafted dark oak door.

The commander kicked opened the door, exposing an angry and surprised Witch who almost dropped her plate of food.

A puff of air leaked from the room...Must that smell of all-things-rotten had to accompany every Witch? How could she even eat in there?

"Ah! Rude spider! Chew, chew..." the Witch barked with her mouth full. "Seely! How many times have I told you to KNOCK? Chew, chew. What junk have you bought me this time?"

Commander Seely was quite used to the Witch's abuse and took no notice of it. He stepped aside to review his find—us—the visitors from Geb.

The Witch's eyes widen at the sight of us.

"You are ahead of schedule." She stood up to invite us into the room. "Seely, go fetch Wilma!"

Seely turned around and slammed the door as he exited the room.

"Ack! These Spiders just have no manners!" the Witch complained.

She introduced herself as Madam Wackrin.

"Where is Wilcara? Isn't she supposed to come here?" Wackrin wasted no time in small talks and her sneering manner was no better than Seely's.

"The enchantment was completed ahead of schedule," the Captain lied. He definitely had the inside scope of the Witches' plans with these world invasion businesses. "We are the scouts. After all, there's no way of knowing where we'll land with this new Obelisk. You must be here ahead of us to tame the cave creatures?"

Wackrin felt no obligation to answer the Captain any question, she looked at us in distrustful eyes and glanced over Kresstan with despise. "You have a Kreepton with you?" She took a closer look, trying to remember if she had seen his face.

"He's an expert scientist." The Captain broke her attention to Kresstan. "We needed advice on how to handle Spiders."

"Fair enough," Wackrin said as the oak door squeaked open again. Another Witch emerged.

"Seely said the Gebs are here?" The Witch who came in was quite excited to see us. She extended a hand to shake the Captain's vigorously. "How delightful! I'm Wilma, nice to meet you all."

"Get a detail report from them," Wackrin shook her head in disapproval of Wilma's exaggeration and ordered the cheerful Witch. "I'll prepare my report to Madam Wilcara."

"Right away!" Wilma said. "Come with me, gentlemen...and lady."

We followed Wilma through another oak door at the back of the room into an office with bookshelves, a table and a few chairs.

The Captain cut right to the questioning as soon as the door closed. "Are the spiders tamed? Is this world secured?"

"I'm afraid I ask the questions first." Wilma smiled but her tone was not at all friendly like she was just a few clicks ago. "Have a sit, Mr..."

"Forgive me, ma'am! I'm Captain Famosa of the Master Hunters, under the command of King Steve." The Captain started over his introduction with a salute. "These two are my subordinates, Hadrian and Augusta, and the tag-along Kreepton scientist."

We saluted too, copying the Captain.

"At ease, Hunters. I have certainly heard of you." Wilma chuckled casually, but she stared at us like spiders taunting their prey. "So where did you land?" She took out a few pieces of paper and conducted her interview with us.

"At a river next to a waterfall. A platform is definitely needed for footing," the Captain answered but popped in his own question. "So, is the return Obelisk built? We do want to get back and report our findings."

"There's one just outside of the nest..." Wilma changed the subject again. "Does Madam Wilcara have any instruction?"

"Just to secure the landing and get a report from

you," the Captain threw in another lie. "So, if you could please show us the way to the surface..."

Wilma stopped abruptly on her note taking and looked at us suspiciously. "Such a rush you are in, Captain."

"Just eager to claim our credits." The Captain played his greedy soldier character well.

Reality was, it wouldn't take long for those in Geb to build another Obelisk and come after us. Whatever we had to do to escape, we had to do it fast.

"You wait here," Wilma said plainly. She went back to the room where Wackrin was.

Her leaving us like that was surely not a good sign.

A small window in the room looked out into the cave of spiders. While the Captain was dealing with Wilma, I saw the spiders brought in pigs and sheep from one of the tunnels just twenty blocks from us. "That could be the way to the ground." I pointed to that tunnel.

"And looks like the rest of us found their way here, too." Kresstan spotted Ella at the mouth of the tunnel we dropped in from. She was swinging another one of her gadgets. "She may be in the process of another reckless move."

And they spotted us too. Lady Kassandra waved conservatively to us behind Ella.

"What does she think she's doing?" The Captain rushed to the window in horror as Ella threw a block with a star-shaped opening in the bottom. The block flew in a u-curve off of Ella's hands and attached itself to the ceiling of the cave. It made a soft but solid "thug" sound.

Their little display certainly attracted the attention of the spiders nearby. They looked curiously to the source of the sound. But before they could react, Ella pulled on a cord that was attached to the block.

From our previous experience with Ella, nothing less than chaos could come out of this inventor's plans and her gadgets. "Prepare yourselves!" Augusta warned. Then again, what we were preparing for? We did not have the slightest clue.

The star block was curiously still at first and the spiders approached it for an attack. Then a sizzling sound began to leak from it and it was growing louder. Sparks started to spring from the star-shaped bottom. Before the spiders had a chance to back away from it, the block exploded! Hundreds of firework rockets shot out of it and went to all corners of the cave.

Chaos.

The once dark dull cave turned into a glorious display of lights. The spiders closest to it were pushed back into the walls of the cave and had colorful fireworks exploded on them. The orbs that escaped the fallen spiders were added to the light show.

In the mist of all that, the remainder of our party lowered themselves down with ropes they probably crafted with spider webs. Remembering the Witches next door, I hopped to the door and pulled out my sword. When I broke down that door of a barrier between us, the Witches were just getting out of the room in response to the commotion.

Their looks of I-know-you-have-something-to-do-with-this told us they were about to attack us. Wilma aimed a potion at me. Kresstan took a shot at the bottle as it barely left her hand and it exploded in front of her face, splashing much of it back on the Witches. The Witches dropped to the ground and couldn't even lift their arms.

"Potion of Weakness." The Captain had been around Witches enough to identify those color liquids by their smell.

"Imposters!" Wackrin sneered. "Wilcara never sent you!"

"Oh, she did, just not in a manner she intended," Kresstan said triumphantly. And in two swift swing of his sword, Kresstan reduced them into orbs and absorbed them.

Outside the room was a sea of fire mixed in colorful glows—those firework cannons already stopped firing, the masses of spiders were either frantically running around as they burned or have already turned into orbs. In the far side of the cave, Councilman Elfen fought his way with a sword towards us in the mount of angry spiders. Ella blasted them into orbs left and right with a rectangular tube with a trigger. Kortess and Kassandra followed them closely and wacked any spiders that the others missed with their pickaxes.

On our side, we fighters rolled into the mass of spiders, joining in the battle to inch ourselves to regroup with our gang.

The two units of invaders finally met up.

"This is insane!" the Captain screamed over all the noise of destruction. A chaotic scene was not exactly what he had in mind.

"We had to take a chance," explained the Councilman. "Who knows how long before your covers are blown."

"No matter," I said as I slayed another spider. "Let's get to that tunnel over there. It could be the way to the ground."

We moved towards the tunnel where the sheep and pigs were taken down into the cave. A few raw pork chops were floating near its entrance. They were probably from the victims of all those fireworks.

The way to get above ground was only a short distance ahead when a familiar white quartz blade descended from the ceiling, blocking our way to the tunnel.

Seely.

Chapter 19:
The Road Back

The fierce Cave Spider Commander did not bother with anymore courtesy. He hissed at us in his spider tongue and pulled out three more quartz blades from his underside. And he was not alone. A dozen more cave spiders, each armed with two blades, surrounded us. Seely's eight eyes turned fiery red, preparing for the right moment to strike. He was determined to take revenge for our disturbance to their orderly existence.

"Fighters, hold them off," the Captain stood his ground in a protective position and whispered to us. "We need to get above ground and locate the Obelisk."

We all knew what to do. My heart was racing. Memories of our Tallect invasion days under the Captain's command flooded my mind. Except this time, we were on the same side as the Kreeptons.

Seely swung one of his four blades forward to commend a group of the spiders to advance towards us. Augusta and Kresstan stepped up to meet them in their path, and quickly reduced them into orbs.

Without another word, Seely drove the sharpen quartz in his right front leg towards the Captain, his left front leg followed suit in a blink. The Captain received the double strong blow with his iron sword and had just enough force to push the revengeful spider back.

The remainder of the eight-legged army joined the battle. We formed a circle and engaged the advancing spiders in all directions.

I assisted the Captain with enduring Seely's high-speed rotating four blades. To our right, Kressatan and the Councilman did their best to hold off the four spiders from breaking through our formation. To our left, Augusta, Kassandra, and Kortess struggled against another four enemies.

Ella pulled out a gadget that looked like a sword with a few buttons on the handle. Its tip sparkled with an electrical charge. Every time she aimed it at a spider, a bolt of lightning shocked her target and temporary paralyzed it, allowing the kill.

Seely's forces pushed us towards the wall of the cave. Though it seemed like we were losing ground, we were, in fact, inching towards the tunnel, which may be our hope to escape. The spiders closed in on us tighter and tighter. By the time Seely realized what our plan was, we had already arrived at the entrance of the tunnel. Ella shocked each of the closest aggressors, giving our team the chance to hop into the tunnel one by one. Seely let out a loud hiss in rage. The force of his blades came at the Captain and me with an increasing magnitude and speed.

Ka-cha.

Ka-cha.

Our swords broke.

Seely chuckled and stood up with his hind legs. He aimed at us to deliver his final blow. The Captain and I hopelessly attempted to defend ourselves with a stick and a piece of cobblestone we managed to pulled out from our inventories.

"Swoosh!" An arrow flew from behind and planted on the exposed belly of the Cave Spider Commander. He dissolved into a cloud and we received the orbs that spilled out.

"We owe you another one, Kresstan!" The Captain turned around as Kresstan aimed at another spider about the attack us.

"Get in!" Kresstan called.

The Captain and I hopped into the narrow opening. After firing his last arrow, Kresstan joined us. The Councilman pushed us pass him in the cramp space, with the spiders not far behind us. Using his skill as a builder, Elfen quickly blocked off the tunnel with his inventory full of cobblestones and thickened the barrier as we moved deeper. At first, we heard digging coming from the other side of the newly placed stones, but as our barrier got thicker, we no longer heard it.

The tunnel quickly became very steep as we moved further in. We had to either dig out steps to climb or pull out some ladders to get up.

After a good thirty blocks or so of vertical climb, at last, we reached the ground above.

It was night. The air was cold, or freezing rather.

We pulled out a few torches to provide us a visual.

A snow biome, or more specifically, we were on top of a very tall mountain that almost reached the clouds!

That spider cave was not a cave after all, but rather a hollowed-out mountain! And that hole we came out of was not the only opening leading into the nest. Before long, spiders were spilling out like black hairy fountains from a few other holes on the mountain top.

The sun was slowly rising on the horizon. Its rays casted a shadow of a tall linear object in the distant, revealing our ticket home—the Obelisk. It was standing on top of an adjacent mountain equaled in size.

"There's a bridge that can take us there." Ella pointed to a one block wide, some thirty blocks long bridge that connected the mountains. She pulled out another one of that star-bottomed firework shooter and readied it. "Just need to get through those spiders."

"Oh, not that again, missy!" The Captain took away the shooter. "This is an open space, those crackers could go anywhere."

The first wave of the black ocean glowing with red eye spots was upon us. "Think fast!" A spider front leg took a shot at Augusta. She managed to push it back and killed it. But another one quickly took its place.

"How about this one!" Ella pulled out a half slab from her inventory. At the press of a button on top, eight blades pop out of its sides like sun rays. She released the horizontal blade block onto the ground, and it started spinning at high speed and migrating towards the black sea of spiders.

"Out of the way!" Ella yelled. "And gang, follow my 'Spindle of Death!'"

That insane Spindle sped down the mountain top in a straight line towards the bridge, cutting down the spiders standing in its path, and clearing us a route to the bridge. We stormed closely behind the Spindle before the wave of spiders drown the route behind us.

With Ella and the Spindle of Death leading the way, we made it to the bridge and speedily crossed it in a single file. Below the bridge was a valley between the mountains some fifty blocks down. A fall of that height would be an instant splash of orbs! The spiders were not ready to let us go. The mass of them wrapped around the bridge in all four sides and followed us closely behind.

As the last of us hopped off the bridge and onto the neighboring mountain top, Ella pulled out the all-too-familiar Stone Vaporizer and aimed at the bridge.

PAM, PAM, PAM, SWOOSH, SWOOSH, SWOOSH!

A section of the bridge disintegrated into millions of tiny particles, and the spiders on top of it surrendered to gravity—colorful little fountains of orbs sprang at the bottom of the valley.

The black sea was now even more determined to swallow us, and the lack of a crossing was not going to stop them. They spilled down to the valley, absorbed the orbs of their fallen comrades as they went, and came for us.

The sun had now risen enough to light up this world. I took a click to look around the seeable distances. Mountains just as big after mountains. The landscape of this world was simply made up of a countless number these mountains and the valleys below them.

"They are all nests!?" Augusta exclaimed.

"Looks that way," the Captain assessed our surroundings. "Let's get out of here before any more of them awake to our presence."

The giant Cobblestone Obelisk was not too far in front of us. Our ticket home! How happy I was to see it!

"Activate the Obelisk!" the Captain ordered, "Quickly!"

Professor Kortess and his daughter went right to work. They dug into the Obelisk and set the TNTs and the electricity generator in place. Councilman Elfen made a scaffold out of dirt blocks all the way to the top and placed a golden sword on the tip of the Obelisk. The spiders were starting to emerge from the edge of our mountain by the time the Councilman got back down.

"Professor, initiate!" The Captain readied himself in a battle stand, ready to engage the enemies. "The rest of you, into the Obelisk!"

The Professor keyed in a few codes on the generator. "Ten clicks till activation!"

The spiders were no more than twenty blocks away.

The Professor ran into the opening of the Obelisk.

Fifteen more blocks to go for the spiders.

Six clicks left on the counter.

Ten blocks.

The Captain dived into the Obelisk opening.

Four clicks.

Five blocks.

The Councilman blocked the opening with cobblestones.

Two.

The spiders are knocking on the stones.

One.

Explosions.

BOOM, BOOM, BOOM, BOOM.

A flash of bright light...

Chapter 20:
The Hidden Stronghold

A square glowing object...

The glow was so blinding. I could barely open my eyes.

It was the sun, at midday.

Trees. Lots of trees.

Sounds of metal clinging with something hard...

I felt a kick to my side. "Hadrian! Get up!" Ella's voice.

I stood up slowly with my head still spinning and found myself in the middle of a battle zone! We were surrounded by spiders still! Did we not leave the Arachnid world?

I picked up one of those white quartz blade dropped by a spider near me and stumbled to balance myself.

"You alright, Hadrian?" Augusta flopped to my side, defending me from the angry cave dwellers.

I shook my head really hard to wake myself up. "Where are we?"

"Back in Geb," Augusta chopped down another spider. "Some of our pursuers tagged along the ride."

"Oh, I hate Obelisk travel!"

I tried my best to keep my balance and fought those fangs of the spiders. Close by, the others were also fighting for their lives with whatever weapons or tools they managed to get their hands on. The number of our foes was overwhelming. Our ratio of ten to one was dreadful and we were losing ground fast.

KA-CHA.

The blade broke! The same dismal sound echoed from Augusta at my side. I can't believe we made it back to Geb just to be finished off out here in the forest.

"Well, it has been a great adventure with you, Hadrian." Augusta offered a hand shake as a few spiders were closing in for the kill.

I looked at her in the eye and grabbed her hand as we readied for our final moments.

Their fangs rose high and in search of a nice spot on our heads for the bite.

SWOOSH!

An arrow disintegrated one of them into a splash of orbs.

And another arrow caught up to one other spider... and another...

A shower of arrows rained down on the spiders with deadly accuracy. In a few clicks, our foes were eliminated. Our saviors emerged from behind the dense forest spruce trunks one by one.

Kreeptons! There was a dozen of them, armed with bows.

"My Prince!" The leader of the archers rushed towards Kresstan and embraced him with all his might. "So, it is true! You lived!"

"Koba!" Kresstan returned the embrace to his good friend from Tallect. "You have no idea how glad I'm to see you amongst the hidden survivors we heard about!"

"You made it!" Koba curtsied to the Prince and the rest of the archers followed suit. "I hope you approved of my welcoming gift, Your Highness."

"It was certainly a pleasant surprise." Kresstan held his loyal friend's hands in gratitude.

The Kreeptons exchanged a few updates in their

Kreepton language. The other members of the Kreeptons joined in and surrounded their royal leader in excitement. At the sight of the reunion, Kassandra and Kortess smiled warmly with tears streaming down their faces.

The Captain was not in the mood to enjoy the moment. He squeezed himself into the crowd of Kreeptons. "Sorry to interrupt, but let's continue this celebration somewhere safer."

"Absolutely! Captain," Koba temporarily subdued his excitement and addressed our lot. "The entrance to our hidden Stronghold is just a short walk away."

We headed towards the setting sun and into the denser part of the forest. Our landing location, as we were told, was some five hundred blocks to the west of the Kingdom of Geb, and the Stronghold was just some one hundred blocks further to the west.

Our party abruptly stopped in front of an ordinary looking spruce tree. Koba pulled out a key and inserted it in the solid body of the tree trunk. The trunk opened like a door! On a closer look, the key hole was actually blended in perfectly with the tree texture, almost invisible to an unsuspecting passerby. The door was made by modifying the very top layer of the trunk with extraordinary precision to mask the key hole and the hinges. Such fabulous woodwork could only be the work of the Zombies.

The tree was hollow like a tube. We went through the doorway one by one and slid down a ladder inside. Koba went in last in case of any unwanted visitor trailing us.

Once underground, a long narrow tunnel continued to guide us. After some twenty blocks, the straight tunnel then stepped upwards until we reached what appeared to be a dead end. Yet again, with a key inserted into the "cobblestone wall," by the hand of another Kreepton, the wall retreated into the ground, granting us entry into the brightly lit, sand stone interior Stronghold of the Tallects.

The Stronghold was a cave divided into a few open levels and packed with all sorts of tools, chairs, and tables. Zombies, Skelees, Kreeptons, and a few Humans busied themselves with every possible labor imagined.

Everyone there had a clear view of anyone who stepped into the Stronghold. At the first notice of the new comers, the Stronghold occupants all froze where they were and went drop-dead silent. They looked at us with disbelieve.

"It's Prince Kresstan!" one Kreepton confirmed their extraordinary sighting of their lost Prince.

The rest unfroze instantly and let out a loud and exciting roar of joy to welcome us.

"Our days of hiding will soon be over!" another Kreepton yelled.

"We shall reclaim our Tallect once again!" cried a Zombie.

Kassandra and Kortess recognized some familiar faces from their comrades at the Settlement. I also spotted two other members of the Master Hunters, a few other citizens of Geb, and Zella!

Koba offered a spot in the center of the Stronghold to the Prince. Kresstan raised his hands to receive his subjects' support. The crowd corporately quieted down to give their undivided attention to their long-lost leader.

An Elder Kreepton handed Kresstan his hard-to-miss enchanted diamond sword of the royals. This treasure was teleported to Geb on the night of the Obelisk explosion and had been kept safe by the survivors in the Stronghold. With the symbol of royal supremacy in his hand, Kresstan began to speak with humbled authority.

"My dear Tallects, I've only recently learned of your miraculous survival. King Steve and the Witches have abused us for far too long!" Kresstan could hardly contain his flood of rage, regrets, and sadness. "I have failed you once due to my inexperience, but I shall not let that happened again!"

The Tallects showed much pride as they listened to the Prince's speech. They cheered and applauded in agreement.

"I cannot thank our Human allies enough for the sacrifices and the risks they took," Kresstan directed the crowds' attention to us. "Without them, I would have fallen victim to the Witches' treachery!"

We Humans received the next round of applause.

"But I regret to tell you that war is not over." The mood in the Stronghold sunk. "Until we are rid of the Witches' control over Geb and our own world, peace would not bestow upon us."

"King Steve and the Witches are no match for our determinations!" someone in the crowd called out. "Lead us to victory!"

Cheers broke out once more.

"Thank you for your trust in me," Kresstan continued after the crowd calmed down slightly. "I can only repay you with my best ability to lead. Together with our Human allies, we shall take back our freedom, and our world!"

The audience responded with great enthusiasm. The emotions in the Stronghold was at its highest. Submerged in a sense of joy and empowerment, preparation for war went underway immediately.

In one corner of the Stronghold, swords were made and sharpened. In another, bows and arrows were crafted by the dozens. Blacksmiths hammered vigorously on the iron to create tough armors. And all those fit to fight stretched out their limbs to warm up for the big battle.

While the Tallects worked, we took a moment to orient ourselves in the Stronghold. It was built by hollowing out a mountain, forming a cave. A few balconies covered by trees and bushes served as lookouts. The whole structure camouflaged so well that it blended perfectly into its surroundings.

Standing on the top level of the Stronghold, the majestic city walls of Geb was visible just on the horizon. It was a strike-back force hidden in plain sight! I bet the Witches didn't see that coming.

As the leader once again, Kresstan's undivided attention was requested as soon as he settled in. He was kept busy receiving the briefings from everyone. Amongst the briefers was a familiar face that we had met at the Settlement.

"Elder Kossac!" Kresstan recognized the old Kreepton.

"My Prince." The Elder held the Prince's hands in his and took a good long look at the royal Kreepton.

Finding the survivors reminded Kresstan of a very important thing that was lost on the night their ancient Obelisk was set off.

"Pardon me for rushing into business," Kresstan said nervously. "Tell me, are you in possession of the Desert Crystal?"

"Certainly," Elder Kossac's answer relive the Prince of his tenseness. He pulled out a translucent blood-red block from his inventory and handed it to the Prince.

"Thank the Lord of the Block!" Kresstan's eyes glowed with the Crystal at the sight of it. "It did make it to Geb!"

"Unfortunately," Kossac continued, "it doesn't seem to work in this world. We have been unable to spawn anyone."

"So, it needs to be back in Tallect," Kresstan thought as he gently touched the magical block. "We will make that happen! Once we are back, we'll regrow our population and rebuild our civilization."

"All in good time, my Prince," said Elder Kossac gently.

∞ꔙꔙꔙꔙꔙꔙꔙꔙꔙꔙꔙ∞

In the midst of all these preparations for war, the Tallects and the Humans were once again in conflicting positions. After all, it was our own people that we were going to fight.

"Now that we are close to war, I have to consult your opinions." Kresstan found Captain Famosa and the Hunters at a work station. "You have helped us so much and I know there are good citizens in there. I surely do not wish harm to come their way."

"Sometimes wars are necessary to bring order," the Captain said indifferently.

"Is war the only way to go?" Augusta was concerned. "There must be better ways to handle this other than risking more innocent lives."

"What would you suggest?" Kresstan was opened to new ideas.

"Perhaps negotiation?" Augusta suggested. "If there are Humans like us who want to help, they would rather just hand over the Witches...I mean, that's what we want, right?"

"You are too soft!" Captain Famosa snapped. He had his mind fixed on the use of force. "The people of Geb have been so brainwashed to believe the Witches were the victims and Geb 'saved' them. Besides, if a war is what the Tallects want, then a war they will have. Are you so naïve to think you can play good guys on both sides? We chose our sides and we stick to it!"

"I can't express my gratitude enough, Captain," Kresstan addressed the Captain's determination. "But Augusta has a point. Tallects do not wish to end our suffering with suffering of others. A war certainly should be the last resort."

"Great achievement takes great sacrifice," the Captain spoke intensely. "Do not lose sight of your goals now, Prince."

"You have a point. I will consider my options," Kresstan thought deeply.

The Captain had a look of disappointment on his face, but he had no choice but to abide by the Prince's leadership in this matter. However, he did not back down without a warning. "Do as you wish, Prince. It is your people that you have to answer to if you do so fail them again." The Captain casually took a bow and excused himself from our conversation.

Later that day, we saw the Captain caught up to Elder Kossac, who was giving out orders in the back of the Stronghold.

Augusta and I were in a small workroom nearby and couldn't help but to overhear the conversation.

"Elder Kossac, I have fulfilled my promise to deliver your Prince," Captain Famosa cut to the chase and got to his point right away. "Certainly, I can expect that you can guide your Prince to execute your side of the deal."

"There are no other ways for us but to defeat the Witches. We all know, failure would mean death," Elder Kossac responded. "The Witches would not tolerate those who defy them. The Prince knows that."

"But he is showing signs of uncertainty towards war," said the Captain.

"The population of Tallects was greatly reduced after the run in with you Hunters, we have every right to be concerned about the potential casualties of a war!" The Elder was losing his politeness towards the Captain.

"My apologies," the Captain realized he had crossed the line. "Our goals are nevertheless the same."

"Have trust," said the Elder. "I assure you, we will choose a course of action that would benefit us both. And you will have what you desire, given that we come out victorious."

What did the Captain want from the Tallects? Were the Elder and the Captain working behind Kresstan's back? Could the Captain have a different agenda in mind or was he simply being the military man and desired war?

Chapter 21:
The Siege in the Night

The preparation for war went on for three more days, until everyone, Tallects and Gebs, had a full set of iron armor and some sturdily crafted weapons. Ella serviced her radical-but-proven-useful gadgets and showed a few brave Tallect ladies how to use them. The Tallect army, though small, looked quite impressive and intimidating.

We found out that there were some thirty members of the Underground Network. The actual number was unknown since each member only had a few immediate contacts for secrecy reasons. In case they were captured and interrogated, they would not be able to provide more than a few names. It would take longer to do all that detective work to catch every member, allowing most members to escape. The Network had infiltrated different positions in Geb's society. That was how they were able to rescue all the Tallects in the different parts of the Kingdom all at once.

Many of the Network members escaped with the Tallects, but some of them took the risk of staying in the City to be spies. A Master Hunter by the name of Sulfur was in charge of keeping contact with the spies in the City.

"Our spies had reported that after your grand escape with the Obelisk, the City has gone into shock," Sulfur informed Kresstan and the other leaders at the Stronghold. "People are afraid to go out of the City. Everyone retreated inside the inner walls to strengthen the security. The inner city gates were locked and heavily guarded. A new Obelisk did get built, and a few Witches had gone to the Arachnid world to come after you. Needless to say, they would come back empty handed. King Steve had since then, mobilized his own army to prepare to take on the escaped Tallects. Citizens are requested to donate as much of their XP orbs as possible to enchant the army's weapons."

All that suggested an uphill battle for us.

However, we had two advantages: one, we had the element of surprise. Geb had no idea what to expect or when to expect us; and two, much of Geb's citizens had never seen war. Their relative inexperience would leave them distressed and confused while facing our army.

"Master Hadrian and Master Augusta are labeled as traitors and said to have schemed with the Tallects," Sulfur further stated. "But the King wouldn't dare to disdain your name, Captain. You are too much of a hero to be labeled as a traitor. The people rather believe you were taken against your will at the Obelisk."

"That's excellent news," said the Captain. "We can certainly use that to our advantage."

After some careful consideration, the leaders had reached a consensus on a plan that would achieve our goal and minimize our casualties.

Everything was ready. We were set to siege the City the next day.

The night before our big battle was tense. It went by slowly. The Tallects, who did not need sleep, made the final preparations quietly, while the Humans tried hard to get some rest.

At sunrise, armors and weapons were distributed. Kresstan delivered his speech to the geared-up soldiers.

"Tallects, this is our chance to claim all that are due to us! We shall bring those traitor Witches to justice and take our home back!"

The Tallects drummed their weapons and let out a thundering war cry.

At noon, they marched. The army of some one hundred Tallects and Humans marched out of the Stronghold, through a total of five tunnels hidden deep under the forest canopy, and emerged from five different disguised trees like the one we entered the Stronghold from. It was as if we appeared out of thin air!

By late afternoon, Kresstan's army had marched through the unguarded outer wall without any resistance. They regrouped in a clearing amongst the woods on the western hills just outside the city wall.

The setting sun behind us casted a long shadow on the army, making everyone appeared taller. Together with the darkening sky, under limited visibility, the relatively small army at the gate appeared much larger and more mysterious.

The soldiers on top of the city wall trembled in fear at the sight of the trespassers. A few took off and headed into the City, likely in order to inform the King of our arrival.

The Captain, Sulfur, Augusta and myself observed the demonstration from some forty blocks away behind a tree. As intimidating as the siege seemed, it was merely a decoy. The army was meant to serve as a bargaining power to buy time. While Kresstan distracted Geb by asking for the King and negotiating for peace, the Hunters would be allowed to carry out our real mission: capturing the Witches with minimal damages to Geb.

We applied dye we gathered from our surroundings on our faces to further disguise ourselves from being recognized. As much as we would like to fight alongside our friends, we had a more importation mission to accomplish.

"The guards are distracted and are gathering at the Gate," Captain Famosa whispered. "Now is our chance."

We approached that towering city wall of ten blocks high. Aiming at the top, Sulfur threw a hook attached to a strong rope made from those webs we collected from all those spiders we killed. The Captain led our stealth climb up the wall.

"Good luck, friends!" I whispered to myself and gave one last look at the Tallect army before making my climb.

That section of the wall was almost deserted. One low-ranking guard stood there anxiously, watching his comrades rushing to the commotion. He did not even hear the hook clink. The Captain swiftly climbed up the wall, sneaked up behind the unsuspecting guard and tapped him lightly with the "Red Stone Snoozer"— another of Ella's handy work—and the guard was out cold on the ground.

The rest of us followed the Captain closely behind.

"We fight to claim back our freedom. Not to take lives." I faintly heard Kresstan's announcement to the guards in the distance. And how many lives we would be able to save depended on how fast we could get through the City.

Darkness was fast upon us.

We slipped past the unconscious guard and looked into the City on top of the wall. Seemed like the news of "enemy at the Gate" had spread in lightning speed. Crowds of panicking citizens dispensed as they caught the news and further carried it into every block in the City, passing on panic like a plague.

"We need to hurry!" the Captain said as he led the way down the city wall by a ladder nearby. "Before these silly people hurt themselves too badly."

We rushed through the streets in the City. Citizens were either running into hiding or gearing up for war. Our fast pace blended in perfectly with everyone. Nobody paid attention to us in this hectic scene.

Swiftly, we reached our destination of the Garrison. The Captain pushed open the Garrison's iron gate with force. The noise attracted the attention of the soldiers. The frantically busy soldiers were occupied with arming themselves and were annoyed by the intrusion.

"You are not allowed in here, sir." A soldier closest to the gate waved us out as he put on his helmet. "A battle is about to start."

"No! There isn't going to be one if I can help it!" The Captain wiped off his face paint and we followed.

The soldiers froze in place and took a few clicks before they could utter a word.

"Captain Famosa... And the traitors!" The soldiers were shock at our presence. "The King announced your inevitable death in the hands of those Tallect sympathizers..."

"I'm very much alive and those two are no traitors!" the Captain spoke with his powerful commending voice. "We have all been deceived like fools. But I'm going to make sure we fix things right and hunt down our real enemies. So are you with me or not?"

"Sir...I...We..." One of the soldiers shook his head to rid of his confusion and straighten up his posture. "Sir, YES, SIR! I'm at your service!"

The others, seeing the example, saluted the Captain in unison. The Captain sure had a tremendous influence over Geb's armed forces, perhaps even more influential than the King himself. The soldiers stepped aside to give way to the Captain and we headed to the barracks to gather the other soldiers.

At the cracked open of the barrack door, noises as loud and muddled as a marketplace poured out and flooded our ears. The inside of the barracks looked nothing like a proper military establishment...

Young soldiers were frantically running around like scared chickens. They stumbled to orient themselves and searched for their gears as if it was the first time they stepped foot in there. Metal items slipped off hands like wet soap and flew across the room. No one was even aware of our presence. The whole place was a totally disorganized mad house—a clear sign for lack of commend.

Peaking from behind the Captain, we were not sure if we should laugh...

"This is what happens when I'm not around..." The Captain sighed in disapproval. He roughly pushed his way through the half-dressed-childlike soldiers and climbed up to a chest.

"ATTENTION!" The Captain's loud confident voice stood out as clear as a TNT explosion in the middle of scrambled blocks. The soldiers were alerted and looked to their commander.

"Captain Famosa!" a soldier exclaimed. "But you are supposed to be..."

"ENOUGH OF ME BEING DEAD!" the Captain barked. "I am standing right here! And I'm taking back control over your pea brains! Now you are either going to obey me or I'll break you down into orbs RIGHT NOW!"

"I'm with you, Captain!" a Master Hunter in the crowd squeezed his way to the Captain and took the lead in responding.

"So am I!" another soldier said.

And just there, we had the forces for our mission.

We lined up the soldiers in the open area of the Garrison so that everyone could hear the Captain's orders.

Cheers roared throughout the Garrison as the news of the Captain's returned passed around. The soldiers assembled at the open area chanted the Captain's name.

"Our brave and invincible Captain Famosa has returned!"

"ATTENTION!" The Captain abruptly cut short the celebration. "I'm glad you chose my side. Your loyalty shall be rewarded soon enough. But first, we need to clear Geb of an immediate threat..."

Chapter 22:
The Chamber of Doom

The new moon was nearing the top of our heads. Citizens had either headed to the Gate to face off the Tallects or had hidden in their homes for safety, leaving much of the City dark and quiet.

Under the shield of the night, six teams of soldiers led by Master Hunters headed out into the City quietly. The torches in their hands dimly lit their ways. Their mission was to hunt their "preys" in the City without alarming the others.

Their prey: the Witches.

At the same time, Captain Famosa left the Garrison with the majority of the soldiers. They headed towards the Western Gate to take control of the situation over there. If Kresstan's stalling went well, The Tallects and Gebs should still be locked in a staring contest in the dark. Per Kresstan's request, the soldiers were not supposed to fight and wait for King Steve to show up and negotiate.

But the King would never make it to the Gate if we could help it.

Sulfur, Augusta, and I were in charge of the most important mission—to capture the King and his sidekicks, Wilcara and Wicka. With them as our proof, we could expose the Witches of their true intentions to rule over Geb to the people.

Armed with a scroll bearing the Captain's seal of approval, Sulfur held the authority of the Kingdom's military commander. We should have no trouble persuading the other soldiers to join us.

As we neared the entrance of the Castle, flashes of lights broke out in the direction of the Northern Gate. It was likely the result of the rapid throwing of potions.

"The fight has begun between the Witches and one of our teams," said Sulfur. "It won't be long before the King and his Witches know what's happening."

At the grand golden doorway of the Castle, a few guards were keeping watch. Sulfur rushed up to them and swung the scroll opened to display the Captain's seal.

"I have orders from Captain Famosa! You are to obey without questions!" shouted Sulfur. His urgent manner rendered the guards speechless. They were not sure what to make of three Master Hunters and a group of soldiers at the Castle when we were expected at the Western Gate facing off the invaders.

"Follow me to arrest the traitors of Geb!" Sulfur's demand confused the guards even more, as Augusta and I, the proclaimed traitors, were right in front of them.

Master Sulfur did live up to his name. He certainly had the personality of the key component in gunpowder—it didn't take much to ignite his rage. No doubt every soldier in Geb knew Sulfur was not one who had patience. The guards hastily followed the order. They signaled a few more equally confused guards we encountered along the way to join us.

Our growing party leaped up the flights of staircases to the Grand Hall without any resistance. Two guards stood guard at the magnificent jeweled door at the back of the Grand Hall.

"Is the King in there?" Sulfur asked, still breathing heavily from our race up the stairs.

"Yes... Master Sulfur, sir..." one of the guard answered while nervously checking out the dozen or so soldiers and guards occupying the Grand Hall. "But His Majesty ordered us not to disturb while he prepares to meet those Tallects at the Gate."

"By the order of Captain Famosa, King Steve and the Witches are to answer for crimes they committed against Geb." Sulfur pulled out the scroll once more, while waving his sword dangerously close to the face of the guard. "So step aside or I WILL LIGHT THIS PLACE UP WITH PIECES OF YOU!"

Sulfur was in no mood to allow the guards to take their time in deciding. He pushed them aside, yanked that heavy jeweled door open, and stepped right in to the King's Private Chamber.

King Steve's Private Chamber was said to be the safest and the most luxurious place in Geb. Only a few had the privilege to set foot in there. Even the Captain had only heard rumors of the beauty behind the jeweled door.

And now, we were about to go in.

Augusta and I stepped through the door closely behind Sulfur, expecting to see a chamber no less decorated as the door that concealed it.

To our astonishment, the space behind the door was pitch black!

Darkness surrounded us. After our eyes adjusted to the dim light coming from the door behind us, we could see that a single-block-wide stone bridge was the only ground in front of us. Below was an infinite drop into a void. A giant rectangular prism was floating in midair about ten blocks out form the door.

"Watch your steps," Sulfur warned and pulled out a torch to provide some desperately needed security. "It's not called the 'safest' place in Geb for nothing."

Safest for the occupant, indeed. Uninvited guests shall enter at their own risk.

We proceeded slowly into the void in a single file. It was the longest ten blocks I had ever traveled! The soldiers behind us were so focused on staying on the bridge that no one made the slightest sound.

A single solid iron door ended the walkway and served as the entrance to the floating prism, but there was no button.

After we touched and felt every block surrounding the door using the limited light from Sulfur's torch, cautioned ourselves not to slip, Augusta noticed a bump to the right side of the block underneath Sulfur. "I think I found it."

At the push of the button, the door opened. The creaking of the door's hinges echoed in the empty space so loudly that those inside the Chamber were instantly alarmed.

The moment Sulfur stepped foot in the Chamber, a flask of potion flew straight at him. Sulfur's quick reaction and swift moves allowed him to catch the flask and keep it from breaking. He threw the potion back at its owner.

The iron door closed behind Sulfur.

I quickly hit the bottom again and rushed into the Chamber with Augusta.

A few more potions headed our way! But Sulfur was quick enough to catch them too and saved us.

At a quick assessment of the Chamber, the seemingly isolated space did have another way out. Across the room, King Steve and Wicka were busying themselves with removing some furniture to reveal a trap door on the ground. Wilcara was in their company. She pulled out a few more potions from her inventory and started rapidly firing them away at us.

The iron door opened again.

A few soldiers that just entered through the iron door were not able to dodge the flasks. The effects of the potions knocked off their balance and they fell back and slipped off the bridge into the void.

The iron door closed.

"KING STEVE! There's no point in running!" Sulfur shouted to the escapees. "Captain Famosa will expose who you and your Witch friends *really* are to the people!"

"So I should let you arrest me?" the King laughed as he hopped down the trap door.

Sulfur moved towards the trap door but Wicka stood in the way and held up her stock of potions. "We have to get going now. Since we've got no time to throw a farewell party, let me throw *these* instead!"

Joined by Wilcara, the Witches resumed their potion attacks. The smell of potion in the air was suffocating.

Even as quick as we were, it did not take too many more broken flasks before we succumb to their power......

All the noises faded...

I was alone in the Chamber...

This space belonged to me...

I was too occupied by the chaos earlier to even notice how beautifully white this place was. Instead of overly decorated with precious stones, the room was built with simple white quartz blocks from the floor to the ceiling. A roll of glowstone half way up the five-block tall wall lighted the space.

The edges and corners were so straight, so square and angular...

Then something was happening to one of the corners of the ceiling. It was collapsing inward! The straight edges were disappearing! The same was happening to the other corners of the Chamber and the dismay is spreading.

The whole room was starting to turn into one of the most horrifying things in the block world—A SPHERE!

Smooth with infinite number of edges, the floor was rounding up and the whole sphere Chamber was closing in on me! Where the Chamber touched me, my own edges melted away. I was infected with the curve too!

I could hardly breath, move, or see...

"Ahhh..." I heard myself screamed helplessly...

"Hadrian!" Augusta's voice echoed faintly. "Wake up! Get a hold of yourself! It's not real!"

Not real......

The potions......

Right!

I closed my eyes and tried my best to calm myself and focus.

When I opened my eyes, we were still in the same rectangular prism Chamber. A few more soldiers managed to get inside, but everyone was either slow moving or appeared quite lost in their delusions.

"Blasted blocks! That was a whole load of potion of nightmare and mining fatigue!" Sulfur shook his head vigorously to regain control of himself.

"The King and the Witches?" I oriented myself and quickly turned to the direction of our assailants.

They were already down the trap door. With one last high pitch laugh, Wicka closed the trap door above her head. The closing of the trap door was followed by the sound of a lever's click... and the sizzling sound of an ignited TNT...

"Darn fatigue!" Sulfur grumbled. "I would very much like to run now!"

Shaa-shaa-BOOM! BOOM!

I couldn't look...

Shap...shap...shap...

When it all quiet down, I was quiet amazed to be alive! We were all alive!

The iron door opened again, the last of our party finally got in.

"The King's Chamber is a desert?" a newly entered soldier observed.

"No," Augusta pointed to a big hole in the ceiling blocked up by sand that piled from the floor up. "Looks like the explosion released a ton of sand, covering up the trap door."

"It's preventing us from pursuit! What a bunch of cowards!" Sulfur pounded his fist on his hand in anger. But he quickly called on his wit and sent his team to handle the present situation. "We need to remove this pile of sand to go after those traitors and bring them to justice!"

"Yes, sir!" the soldiers answered in unison. They pulled out a few shovels and tackled those lose yellowish substance. But there seemed to be no end to it, another block quickly fell in from the hole as soon as we removed one at the bottom.

My inventory was quickly filling up with stacks of sand. I mumbled to myself as I tackled them. "Risky bridge, narrow iron door, escaping trap door, shower of potions, and piles of sand. How much worse can it get?"

And why did I have to jinx it?

"Something is moving in the sand, sir!" One of the soldiers backed up from the stack he was working on.

"Non-sense! What could possibly be..." As Sulfur approached the spot where the soldier indicated, the whole pile started to crumble down. A six or seven block tall moving chain of sand blocks separated itself from the rest of the sand blocks, and it was growing longer.

"Everyone, back up!" Augusta called.

We backed into the walls of the chamber as far away from the creature as possible.

"What in my square bottom is that?" Sulfur pulled out his bow and signals the rest of us to take aim at the creature. "On my mark...ready...FIRE AT WILL!"

A few dozens of arrows pierced the creature, but none seemed to damage it. The arrows sunk into its sandy body and got flushed out at its bottom. It was like shooting into flowing water.

The creature crawled out of the sand pile that buried it and started to take shape. It was a giant worm composed of blocks of sand!

It certainly did not appreciate a bunch of arrows violating its space. Five tube-like tentacles began to grow out of its head. A pair of glowing green eyes rolled out at the end of each of those tentacles. They began scouting the Chamber for its offenders.

"Steady..." Sulfur raised his sword, preparing for...we

didn't really know what.

Attracted by Sulfur's voice, the creature positioned one of its tentacles above Sulfur's head.

SHAAA......

Blocks of sand shot out of the tentacles and fell straight down onto Sulfur.

The Master Hunter's agility was able to save him from being buried. But the creature was not done making its moves. The tentacle traced Sulfur's movement and continuously spilling out sand onto its target.

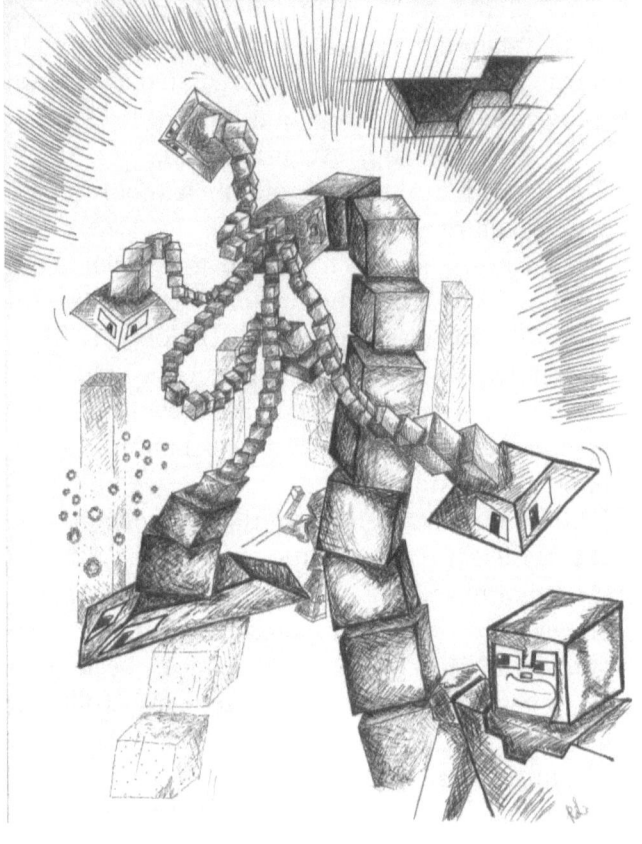

The rest of the tentacles didn't stay quiet for long. They each found a target to track. A few of the soldiers were not quick enough to dodge the suffocating sand and were buried alive. Even the orbs they spilled weren't able to escape and got swallowed by the thick sand.

Sand covered every corner of the Chamber in no time. The creature couldn't possibly run out of sand, for it absorbed the sand blocks in the Chamber back after dropping them over our heads. All we could do was frantically running away from those tentacles.

Another soldier couldn't keep up...

"Get out of here!" Sulfur ordered as he ran. The creature was still in hot pursuit of its first target.

But our hope of escaping quickly vanished. As one of the soldiers reached the iron door, he fell victim to the creature's deadly pursuit. Him, along with our only escape route, vanished underneath the sand.

"We are sitting ducks," Augusta said as she ran pass me. "If only we could control gravity..."

Wait! That's it! An idea came to me. Gravity!

"Listen!" I stopped my running and yelled across the room. "I have a way..." Augusta ran towards me and pushed me out of the way of a sand pile coming at me.

"Careful! It reacts to sounds!" Augusta reminded me.

"That's right!" I resume my loud voice but kept running to stay unburied. "Stay as far away from it as you can and make some noise!"

"I don't know what your plan is, but it better work!" Sulfur yelled across the Chamber.

"I'm not afraid of you, worm!" one soldier yelled.

"Come get me, no brain!" another screamed.

SHAA... SHAA...

Another one of us gone.

As our numbers went down, the creature could focus

~165~

more on the remaining targets, and the chase got more intense. I needed to act fast.

Once the creature's attention moved away from me, I pulled out a TNT, snugged up to the back side of the creature and placed the explosive right next to it.

"It's going for you, Hadrian!" I heard Augusta's voice.

I was just in time to activate the TNT when the creature spotted me.

SHAA...

Half of me sustained injury from the falling sand, but I managed to get away. But my movement was slowed down, with the next one, I'm a goner...

The tentacle aimed for my head.

SHAA...SHAA...SHAA...

BOOM!

The gunpowder had done its magic!

The explosion created a hole on the floor just big enough for the creature and tens of sand blocks to fall through. The sand monster's tentacles hysterically tried to grab onto something but their efforts were in vain. The deadly monster was flushed down into the darkness below.

The floating feature that rendered the Chamber a death trap became the one weapon that could be used against it.

Chapter 23:
The New King

"Excellent work, Hadrian!" Sulfur gave me a big fist bump.

"Looks like we escaped death once more." Augusta offered me a high five.

The surviving soldiers clapped with all their might.

"We'll celebrate later," said Sulfur. "We still have to finish what we started."

"Looks like the explosion also exposed the King's escape route." Augusta pointed to a hole where the trap door was. It led to a now-damaged stairway down the cliff behind the City.

But with a quick head count around the Chamber, there were only seven of us left after the deadly battle, hardly a force enough to measure up to the Witches' power.

"I think we had enough for one day." I knew our limits. "The lot of us in this sorry state can't possibly pursuit some crazy fugitives capable of creating sand monsters."

"Very true," Sulfur concurred. "We'll hunt them down another time."

The still-trembling soldiers were quite glad to hear that.

"Let us regroup and check on the statues of the other teams," Sulfur commanded.

We dug away the sand that buried the iron door and left the Chamber from the way we came. Back out in the

Grand Hall, we concentrated on listening for fighting sounds from the City, but heard none.

Did we win?

In hopes to get some news, we headed out to the balcony outside the Grand Hall, cautious of any enemies hidden behind the pillars and walls.

It seemed that we were alone.

The Garrison was clearly in sight from the balcony. We successfully used the light signal contraption there to make contact with the Control Room at the Garrison.

Sulfur informed the Garrison that the Castle had been secured and to our surprise, Captain Famosa personally replied us. He had triumphed!

From the height of the balcony, we had a clear view of the City. Geb appeared to be peaceful at the moment, but there were spots of clear damages on the walls and small fires in a few areas of the City. Other isolated battles against the Witches must had raged in the night while we were trapped inside the Chamber.

The sun was rising from behind the Castle. The sky was brightening up the City gloriously in celebration of our victory.

What a night it was!

The Tallects had entered the City and were making their way to the Castle. The Captain told us to gather at the Plaza in front of the Castle. He would announce our accomplishments to the people there.

I bathed in this moment of relief and glory. So, that was it. It was over. We won!

As we were walking out of the Grand Hall, for a moment there, I felt like we were being watched. Perhaps my nerves had yet to calm down?

The Captain arrived at the Plaza shortly with his army and supporters trailing him closely.

Each of our teams reported the details and results of our operations. Turned out that the Captain was able to take over the command of the army at the Gate with ease. He declared the Tallects our ally and sent every capable hand out to join the hunt for the Witches.

The team that went to the Northern Gate had great news too. Despite a few Witches escaped using the newly reconstructed stone Obelisk, the rest of them were either captured or eliminated in their battle. With minimal casualties, some ten Witches were captured alive, their inventories rid of potions. Without those color liquids, they were not much of fighters.

Although the Captain was disappointed in our failure in capturing the three key figures in King Steve's government, he commemorated our bravery in defeating the sand monster and lived to tell the tale.

Realizing the battles were over, Geb's people reluctantly got out from hiding and gathered at the Plaza nervously. They whispered and gossiped, trying to figure out the situation. The Tallects in their full armors standing with the Geb army was definitely alarming to the unknowing Human citizens, not to mention the supposed-to-be-dead Kresstan was amongst them.

Captain Famosa ascended to the platform that was reserved for the King to address the crowd. All his supporters surrounded him below the platform like a powerful display of might.

Ella pulled out a voice amplifier from her inventory and handed it to the Captain.

The crowd of Geb citizens went mute in anticipation of the Captain's speech, but not without shooting suspicious looks towards the Tallects present.

"Citizens of Geb," the Captain spoke with a sympathetic tone that you could almost see tears coming from his eyes. The resonance through the voice amplifier further intensify the passion in his voice. "We have been deceived! These Tallects were never our enemies! On the contrary, they have helped us at a crucial moment in Geb's history. They have freed us from our real enemy—King Steve and those Witches!" Famosa pointed to those Witches in captivity.

People murmur in disbelieve.

"Citizens!" the Captain took back the attention with a rusty voice, pleading for the people's understanding. "I swear on my own reputation that all I say is true. The Witches sought to control Geb through the simple-minded Steve. They tricked us into believing the other Tallects were their oppressors and used our hands to hunt down the Tallects. But by the will of the Lord of the Blocks, some of us have discovered the truth. This last night was vital to our survival. Geb's bravest have collaborated with the Tallects and we have defeated the masterminds behind this trickery—the Witches Wicka and Wilcara."

The crowd gasped at the Captain's claim.

"I understand that this is hard to believe, but we have all been played by those Witches like fools!" exclaimed the Captain. "Many have lost their lives for our struggle to take back control of Geb from those foul beings! Let us remember their sacrifices!"

After a brief moment of silence, the Captain continued. "Regrettably, Steve, Wicka, and Wilcara have escaped. But they are now nothing more than fugitives and can do no harm to us anymore. In the meantime, the rest of the Witches will be put on public trials to answer for their crimes against our worlds. I only asked that you stand behind me and condemn those criminals!"

The whispers in the crowd grew louder and eventually became a noise of hundreds chatting.

This was the hardest judgment the citizens had to pass. Should they believe in Captain Famosa? The Captain had been one known to have great integrity. Who would dare doubt his words? Although Geb did enjoy great prosperity under Steve's rule, they all had eyes to see that the Tallects were living like slaves.

Perhaps it was time to do the right thing...

"I'm with you, Captain!" someone declared.

And more concurred. And the rest of Geb followed.

Geb had deliberated to side with the Captain.

"May I ask?" a voice from the crowd silenced everyone present. "With the King gone, who is the new leader of Geb?"

"The answer to that..." the Captain hesitated.

"If I may have permission from Prince Kresstan of the Tallects, I would like to speak freely on behalf of our kinds," a familiar voice emerged from the Tallect army. Elder Kossac, the Kreepton who talked of a deal with the Captain at the Stronghold, made his way to Kresstan.

"You have kept our kinds safe in my absence, Elder. You certainly have every right to speak for us." Kresstan gave a nod and invited the Elder to climb up the platform.

"I am Elder Kossac, high priest of the Kreeptons," the Elder stood beside the Captain and addressed the people. "To keep peace between our worlds, we need strong leaders. Captain Famosa saw passed the pretentious masks of the Witches and took a great risk in protecting and helping us during our time of despair. For that, we own him our freedom and our lives. I'm certain that Prince Kresstan, the Master Hunters, and all of Geb agree that the Captain has demonstrated great courage, leadership skills, and integrity to be a superior leader. If I may, I would like to propose that the Captain be crowned as the new King of Geb."

The Captain shook his head with a rare coyness. "I cannot... There are far more capable citizens..."

"King Famosa!" a soldier yelled.

"All hale the new King!" another added.

Thundering cheers soon broke out in support of the Captain's rising to Kingship.

Kresstan came up and shook the Captain's hand. "Your people love you. You'll make a great King."

The presumed King Famosa raised his hands to accept his promotion but reserved a hint of humbleness. "I'm honored by your support. If anyone would rather take the throne, I'd be happy to step aside."

All ears on the Plaza stood up in alertness to catch any objection. But all remained so quiet that you could hear a sheep baa from a hundred blocks away.

"It is yours, Captain... I mean, King Famosa," Councilman Elfen said with a smile.

Another round of applause and electrifying cheers.

∞๚๚๚๚๚๚๚๚๚๚∞

Celebration filled our schedules in the next three days. Dances, food, friendly exchanges between the Tallects and Geb citizens took place around the City. For the first time, Humans got to know the real Tallects and all the knowledge they had to offer.

I also had a moment of solitary to reflect on this whole experience. Since we left Tallect, everything was happening so fast, my mind couldn't even process all the events.

An idea suddenly came to me. That "deal" between

Elder Kossac and King Famosa... Were we truly fighting for the Tallects or was this a rebellion, a revolution to overthrow King Steve? Were we simply a part of the Captain's plan for him to become King?

Augusta caught me in deep thoughts while I was resting in my lodge within the Castle.

"Something that concerns you?" Augusta asked.

"Yes," I admitted. "King Famosa...You think he used us to remove King Steve and made himself the hero?"

"That is a very serious accusation!" Augusta was surprised to hear my idea. "But I can see why you think that way. He seemed to have control over every step along the way, like he knew exactly what would happen and what to do."

"And that victory speech that he made, that duet he sang with Elder Kossac, he acted like a completely different person," I said, "like they were leading the people into supporting him as King."

"It did look that way..." Augusta thought for a moment.

"Then again, he couldn't have predicted that we would return with Kresstan," I thought.

"Perhaps that simply sped up his plans?" Augusta said. "I mean, all the XP orbs from the Prince and the extra hands we provided must have helped, like defeating those Witches at the Arachnid World and rescuing the Tallects. And most importantly, Kresstan's presence made commending the Tallects much easier."

"That is true, but I think he had the ability to do all those eventually without us. You saw how he was dealing with Elder Kossac," I argued. "So, what should we do? Expose him?"

"No! Absolutely not!" Augusta warned. "The people of Geb love him. And what can we really say he did wrong? He just did what he had to do to get rid of a tyrant."

"You suggest we do nothing?" I said uncomfortably.

"Geb needs time to recover, people want peace and a strong leader." Augusta pointed out. "If his desire is for the good of Geb, despite the tricks he played, he can be a good ruler too."

Though I did not like the idea of having been a pawn, Augusta had a point. As long as King Famosa did not turn out to be another tyrant, we should support him fully.

Chapter 24:
A New Order of the Worlds

At the end of the celebrations, the Tallects were quite ready to return to their long-abandoned homeland.

But they weren't leaving without something to ensure peace in the future.

A meeting took place at the Grand Hall between the leaders of Geb and Tallect. They signed a treaty that stated: all the inhabitants of the worlds shall be equals and no war shall be waged against one another. Further, there shall be regular visits between our worlds so that we may benefit from our alliance.

In hopes to compensate the Tallects for their suffering at the hands of Geb's citizens, the first order of our new alliance was to send Geb workers to help rebuild Tallect. Two dozens of Geb's expert builders and craftsmen volunteered to assist the Tallects in complying with the treaty.

On the day the Tallects were set to leave for their world, Augusta and I went to bid our Tallect friends goodbye.

The majority of the mob spawners outside the City walls were deactivated since King Famosa took control. Only a few of them were left operating to entertain the hunting enthusiasts. The walkway to Beyond the Northern Gate was rebuilt to be wider and well-lit inside and out.

Remembering the last time we ventured out the Northern Gate, our futures were so uncertain. This time around, we looked forward to a bright future under a new order of the worlds.

It was a beautiful sunny day, the travelers gathered around the Sandstone Obelisk and packed the vast obsidian room. It was like a busy market place.

As they waited for their departure, the Tallects were so excited and could not stop chatting about all the things they would do once they got home.

The Geb workers were equally thrilled. They have only heard of Tallect architectures and were eager to take part in rebuilding them.

We found Kresstan next to the Obelisk, surrounded by his advisers. He dismissed them as soon as he saw us.

"So, it's finally time to say goodbye," I said.

"Indeed..." The Prince was lost for words. "Thank you for all that you've done."

"For I-don't-even-remember how many times, you're welcome!" Augusta smiled.

"My apologies, I do not know how best I could repay

you," Kresstan thought hard.

"Just rebuild that civilization of yours," I said. "Once we get everything in order here in Geb, we would come visit."

"And we expect to get some VIP treatments!" Augusta chuckled jokingly.

"Even royal treatments, if you would accept," the Prince offered.

Just then, we spotted Professor Kortess examining the Obelisk with "worry" written all over his face.

"Something wrong, Professor?" Kresstan inquired.

"Your Highness, I do not wish to spoil the mood..." Kortess thought for a moment and spilled his concern with a grim tone. "I have to bring this to your attention...Although the Sandstone Obelisk is enchanted, it will still deteriorate after so many uses. Being the first of its kind, we have no idea how long it will last. Unfortunately, without the Witches' enchanting and potion-making skills, no one knows for sure if we would succeed in enchanting another Obelisk. Perhaps our scientists will be able to work out the technics, but until then, we have to cherish our trips to each other's worlds, for each may be our last."

That, indeed, was a blow to our joyful mood.

"I am certain that we will find a solution before the inevitable destruction of the Obelisk," Kresstan tried to cheer us up.

"Hey! It's not like we can't use an Obelisk, just not as convenient!" Augusta added.

Everyone brightened up again. "That's right!"

Zella came over to inform us that the Obelisk was ready. With one last wave of goodbye, Augusta and I joined the families of the Geb workers in leaving the obsidian room.

From inside the City, we heard the four explosions and blinding multicolor flashes that glowed from Beyond the Northern Gate. With the settling of that light show, our Tallect friends were finally home.

∞൸൸൸൸൸൸൸൸൸൸൸∞

A few dozen moon cycles passed before we had the chance to see Kresstan again.

Longing to catch up with our friends, Augusta and I traveled with a group of scientists and inventors, including Ella, to visit Tallect for an intellectual exchange. Master Sulfur led the trip as our escort.

That was the first time I experienced the luxury of an enchanted Obelisk, and it was almost pleasant! No blackout, no dizziness. I even had a good view of flying through the sparkling green tunnel lined with "O's" and "l's."

The end of the tunnel exited to a seaside—that same location we landed when we were first sent to hunt down the Tallects. The sceneries remained very much the same, but so much had changed.

Despite all that we had done for the Tallects as of late, a sense of guilt towards the Creeper Wars still lingered like a ghost in our hearts. If Augusta and I, who saw minimal actions, felt it, I couldn't imagine what heavy load was spinning in Sulfur's head as he stood next to us and stared out to the sea with an empty expression.

However uncomfortable it was, we had to come to terms with our past errors and move forward with our futures. With that in mind, we made our way towards the Tallect Capital City.

The hike of some one thousand blocks through a vast grassland and forest took us to a very familiar ground—our old neighborhood!

Augusta and I were curious to see if our modest house was still there. To our surprise, it was turned into a monument of some sort! A sign introduced the site as "The Former Home of Tallect's Heroes: Hadrian and Augusta." The surroundings were transformed into a beautiful dandelion garden to commemorate the Underground Network.

Those we wronged had forgiven us! That was a comforting thought.

According to the Tallects' plan, their Capital City was to be rebuilt on its original site—that desert where we built that Sandstone Obelisk that started it all.

Except, it was no longer a desert when we got there.

As we crossed the river and set foot on the sandy ground, a magnificent red sandstone tower greeted us. A red colored chiseled sandstone wall extended from the tower marked the territory of the Tallect Capital City. We entered through the six-block-tall gate at the bottom of the tower.

"His Majesty's comrades!" A Skelee who stood guard at the gate recognized us. "The royal family would be so happy to see you!"

"Royal family?" Augusta wondered who else was in this "family." Wasn't Kresstan the last of his family?

He escorted our party to the Palace through some quiet streets, careful not to catch any attention from the everyday citizens. "I've got to make sure you get to the Palace in one piece," said the Skelee.

"Why..." I tried to ask.

"Shh... It's better to keep quiet," he said. "Trust me, you would rather stay invisible."

Were there Tallects who would not welcome us here?

We "sneaked" into the Palace from the servant's entrance with hardly anyone noticing. A few Zombies gladly received us and seated us at a large hall with a few tables and a few comfortably cushioned sofas while they went to notify the recently crowed King.

Not long after, Kresstan rushed into the hall and gave us a long, tight welcoming hug. "It's been too long!"

"We miss you too, Kresstan!" said Augusta.

"And look who else is here!" Ella noticed someone else behind the King.

"Oh, yes! Please allow me to introduce my wife, Queen Kassandra, and Princess Kayssa." Kresstan presented his family.

"Lady...I mean Queen Kassandra!" I wholeheartedly admired the regal couple and their small Kreepton child in the Queen's arms. "Your Majesties sure move things along, wasting no time!"

"We've lost enough time already." The Queen smiled sweetly at her love. "Our kinds have suffered long enough and are due their wishes to, once again, have a stable and secured home to raise their families."

Kresstan took his former comrades for a tour of his magnificent Palace, to a meet-and-greet with the new generation of Tallects, and to visit some major buildings in the City.

And then we knew why that Skelee guard wanted us to keep quiet earlier.

Words of our visit had spread in the Capital by then. Our presence sprouted some well-intended turbulences wherever we went! Tallects stormed up to us enthusiastically, especially those young Tallects who had only heard of our legends. They came with gifts for us or just wanted a hand shake. Perhaps it would have helped if we had bigger inventories or more hands. The guards tried their best to keep the crowd at bay. Kresstan laughed uncontrollably as we frantically received the fans surrounding us.

"Well, at lease someone is enjoying himself!" Augusta said as a dozen cakes got deposited into her inventory.

Future inventors bombarded Ella with questions on her prized gadgets. "Three moon-cycles of... red... woodblocks ...circuit... jumping... diamond... chickens..." And she did her best to provide answers to everyone, though not in a particular sensible manner.

It was a heroes' reception. And an ecstasy for the City.

The eventful day finally concluded at the elegant blue sandstone Temple—the place where all Tallects were spawned. Our fans, at last, had to be disbanded to keep peace at the sacred building.

A desperately needed relief for us!

Turned out that Zella and her now-grown-up son, Zee, were overseers at the Temple. After a cheerful reunion, they introduced us to the most vital treasure of Tallect's survival.

"Elder Kossac restored the Desert Crystal on the altar in the center as soon as the Temple was rebuilt," Zella showed us the glowing floating red crystal inside a glass case. "Since then, many Tallects had been spawned."

"The would-be parents would gently place their hands on the Desert Crystal, contributing a few XP orbs each, and a new life would spawn from within," Zee explained.

"Quite miraculous!" I exclaimed at the marvel.

"There are things our science still can't explain..." Ella looked on with her inquisitive eyes.

"It's such an honor to have been a part of restoring this wonderful world and people." Augusta said.

We were guests at the Palace for a few moon cycles, spending whatever time Kresstan could spare us from his busy schedule. We talked, laughed, and remembered our adventures. The Queen and Princess Kayssa were great hostesses in keeping us pretty entertained, too.

In the meantime, Ella and her team of scientists made some substantial exchanges with the Tallects, resulting in perfecting a number of new inventions and designing some new ones. The latest we heard was a blueprint for a machine that could replace the orbs extracting potion.

Sulfur had his fun, too. He had countless duels with any Tallects who dared to challenge him, and won nearly every match.

Our trip was a fruitful one.

Nevertheless, as much as we enjoyed our time in Tallect, it was our duties to be by King Famosa's side. After all this time, the Geb workers who came to help with Tallect's building projects were also longing to head home to their own families.

Before long, the Geb-bounded one-time-use Obelisk was constructed. Ah! The torment of an un-enchanted nauseating transportation! I'm not sure if I wanted to repeat such a journey before someone figured out how they could make the enchantment!

We gathered outside the Capital and got ready to say our goodbyes once more. Putting aside our sadness to leave Tallect again, we were glad to return to Geb knowing that our friends had peace at last.

I took my place within the teleporting radius of the Obelisk, awaiting the explosions. I relived in my head all the wonderful and pleasant experiences we had during this trip—just focus on all the senses that was anything but that horrid landing...

Off we went...

And landed, we did...

"AHHH!! Get those spiders off me!" My arm felt like it was getting yanked by those sharp clamping mouths.

"Hadrian!" I heard Augusta's voice, "It's just a tree!"

A Tree?

I squinted my eyes real hard to focus my vision.

Of all the possible blocks I could land on, I landed on a tree! And one of my sleeves was caught on a branch, leaving me hanging there in midair.

I set my arm free and dropped to the ground with a solid perfect landing. But that didn't save my face one bit.

On our way back to the Kingdom, Ella could not stop making fun of my one annoying weakness. Sulfur was not helping by coming up with all kinds of training ideas that may help me overcome the side effects of the Obelisk.

"I seriously don't think throwing ten Ender Pearls at once does the same thing as an Obelisk..." I objected to one of Sulfur's ideas. "I really don't want to be split in ten pieces..."

"Oh, you are just worried that weak stomach of yours can't handle those powerful rare jewels!" Ella mocked.

I shot her a how-dare-you-tease-a-Master-Hunter look and just ignored her.

By now, I noticed that the Obelisk had a much stronger effect on me compared to the others for reasons

I had yet to understand. But one thing I knew: I absolutely hated traveling with the non-shiny version of those giant pillars!

Back in the City, it didn't take long for us to settle back into our routine as our old soldier-selves—daily training exercises, meetings with the Council, and mingling with the Citizens. We moved into a house five times the size of our Tallect lodging and enjoyed our respectable Master Hunter status amongst the elites of Geb.

Life was peaceful again.

In the days to come, King Famosa continued the search for Steve and the Witches. He offered a handsome bounty for any information leading to their arrest. Yet, the fugitives remained at large. Despite this little imperfection, the citizens of Geb resumed their joyous lives and enjoyed what our world had to offer.

So, there it was, a happy ending to our story.

Little did we know, Steve was not finished with the troubles that followed him...

 Epilogue

Steve, now stripped of his crown and influences over his people, took refuge with the escaped Witches, Wilcara and Wicka. They constantly moved from hideout to hideout to avoid being captured by the victors. The Hunters who used to hunt down Tallects had switched to targeting those three.

Without the people's support, Steve was of no use to the Witches, and they quickly got tired of babysitting him. As soon as they got beyond the reach of their enemies, they confronted the former King with their true colors.

Wicka stopped in front of Steve's path. "The time we worked together was great, Steve, but I'm afraid it's time for you to move on and be on your own."

"But...but where will I go?" Steve complained. "I don't have a home anymore. And I'm now a fugitive thanks to *your* failed scheme!"

"You blame us? Your people deserted you because of your incompetence!" Wilcara deflected Steve's blame.

Understanding that he was in a weak position, Steve switched his tactics to begging. "Please, consider all that I've done for you, you have to take me with you to wherever you are going! I'm sure I can still be of use!"

"Unfortunately, where we are going, you won't be needed." In a slick motion, Wicka flung a potion of stiffness at Steve's feet. Steve couldn't react quickly enough to the attack. He was frozen in place. "But no worries, we'll take care of you first..."

"No...no...!" Steve struggled to break free but his body was not responding to his will.

Wicka slowly approached Steve with a wicked grin and pulled out a sword from inside her robe. "Shall we do this fast or slow?"

"You don't...don't have to do this!" Steve tried to make his final plead but could only watch in horror as Wicka lifted up the sword and aimed straight for him.

As the blade was coming down for Steve, out of nowhere, drops of eerie purple sparkles sprinkled on them. Wicka instantly abandoned her killing thoughts and withdrew in fear.

"Endermen!" Wilcara was alarmed and searched frantically for sightings of those dark evasive creatures.

Steve regained his freedom while the Witches were distracted. Seeing that he was temporary neglected, Steve took the opportunity to slip into a group of bushes nearby. His hint of curiosity kept him in the neighborhood to see what it was that the Witches were so afraid of.

The Witches couldn't care less about Steve anymore. Wicka switched her sword into a defensive position and handed a few potions to Wilcara. A dense fog started up around them and covered the sun. Day turned into night instantaneously. The purple sparkles grew in numbers.

The Witches shook in fear. "Come out now! You Endermen!" Wicka called into the fog, trying to rid herself of the fear.

A pair of deep red eyes blinked in the mist of the fog.

"Those aren't Enderman eyes..." Wilcara said nervously.

"But the Endermen are certainly here!" Wicka looked around and noticed that they were cornered by no less than a dozen Endermen standing just a few blocks from them.

A mouth split opened in midair below those red eyes. "Ah, Witches! Always trouble no matter which world it is!" the mouth said. "Perhaps it was a mistake to create your kind."

"You are ... The Creator?" Wilcara could hardly believe the presence of this all-powerful-mysterious-formless being.

"So you know about me too?" the mouth of The Creator said.

"You bet I do. Witches know a lot of things." Wilcara was feeling proud of her knowledge of the worlds. "You are the one who created the worlds and designed all the creatures in it!"

"Yes, and the role of the Witches is supposed to bring order and balance to the inhabitants of the worlds." The Creator's eyes stared down at Wilcara with annoyance. "But the likes of you have such tendency to abuse the knowledge that you have access to and create all sorts of problems."

"We did bring about order and prosperity!" Wicka said in defense.

"By linking the worlds together!?" The Creator barked. "That is not part of *my* design! You were simply consumed by your ambitions to rule over the worlds!"

"We...we..." Wilcara could not contest to the statement about their true intentions.

The Creator knew his creatures well.

"You really think you can do everything you want in my absence?" The features of The Creator floated up close to the Witch's face. "And you dare stealing my sand monster prototype!"

"Borrow! Just borrow!" Wilcara attempted to justify their offense. "Give it a test, to show you how amazing of a creation it is! Didn't it get rid of those Hunters?"

"The last I checked, they were still very much alive and enjoying their victory."

"They survived that death trap of the Chamber?" Wicka exclaimed in disbelieve. "You are lying!"

"Why would I lie to one about to get deleted?" The Creator said with a chilling smile.

"Deleted...?" Wicka panicked. "No, you don't have

to do that!"

"What? Let you respawn again? Dream on!"

"There's still much use we can be to you!" the Witches tried their luck at one last bargain. "The Master Hunters, they know too much! That Kreepton Prince... and... and..."

"No matter. I'll clean up the mess myself," The Creator sighed. "Starting with the two of you."

The pair of red eyes faded into the fog as Endermen closed in to take their place...

"NOOO......!" The cry of the Witches echoed in the forest.

Moments later, the fog cleared up. The Witches and the Endermen were no longer in sight. Two streams of orbs shot up into the sky from where the Witches were standing. Hundreds of orbs rained down. But before they could reach the ground, they evaporated like puffs of air.

To be continued......

The Inspiration

Like many boys his age, my son is a big fan of Minecraft. One Halloween, we decided to build some life-sized Minecraft objects out of cardboard boxes for our decorations. Among them was a four-foot-tall Creeper.

After a night of fun, the Creeper, along with some Jack-o-lanterns remained standing on our front porch for months. Then I wondered, what could it possibly be doing there? And the story of the Kreeptons was born.

Renee Libra

www.ingramcontent.com/pod-product-compliance
Lightning Source LLC
Chambersburg PA
CBHW030225180626
46810CB00008B/2968